Mary Cunningham

Cynthia's Attic:
The Missing Locket

Book One

Echelon Press
9735 Country Meadow Lane 1-D
Laurel, MD 20723
www.echelonpress.com

First Echelon Press paperback printing: December 2005

10 9 8 7 6 5 4 3 2 1

Cover Art © Nathalie Moore
2005 Arianna Best in Category Award winner

Editor: Elizabeth Baird

Printed in USA

Dedication

To my granddaughter, Brittany.

Acknowledgement

Special thanks to my husband, Ken, for his encouragement and support.

To my best friend, Diana, for always being there. Thanks to Diana and Melinda, my first editors, and to Pat and Ruben for all your help and support.

Thanks to Echelon Press and Karen Syed for seeing something special in *Cynthia's Attic*. It was a pleasure working with Betsy and Kat who actually made editing fun!

Special thanks to my dad, who gave me compassion and creativity. And last, but not least, to my childhood friend, Cynthia, and my "guardian angel," Gail.

Prologue

Cynthia had an attic. Not just an ordinary attic. Cynthia's attic was magic.

Cynthia and I came into the world just three months apart. We grew up on the same quiet, sycamore-lined street, our friendship as close as our houses. Fifty years earlier, our grandmothers were best friends. However, we didn't realize the extent of their friendship until after our experience in Cynthia's attic. This is the story of one of our great adventures...the way I remember it.

Chapter One
1914

Her long, slender fingers lay motionless on the keys of the mahogany grand piano as she thought about her family...and of a precious possession. "Will it ever be found?" she whispered aloud, her eyes becoming transfixed on the flickering of the brass candelabra. She had been certain that by now the secret would have been unlocked, but time was running out. *There is still a chance, if only the two young girls find the way to connect to the past...her past.*

1964

"Hey, Cynthia," I yelled as I rounded the corner of her house, squinting in the morning sun as it glared off the white clapboards. Shoving a huge wad of Bazooka bubble gum to the opposite side of my mouth, I managed to continue, "Hurry up! You're the only one with a catcher's mitt."

"Oh, Gus," Cynthia whined, fussing with her pink chenille robe as she hung halfway out the window, "do I have to play? You know I'm no good at softball." Craftily changing the subject, she added, "I just got that new *Beatles* record today. C'mon up and listen to it."

That sure sounded tempting…but no, I stood my ground. "You promised, Cynthia," I demanded, kicking a big clump of dirt off the sidewalk and back into the flowerbed. "Tell ya what, just play for a little while and then I'll listen to your stupid record."

"Oh, all right." She sighed, disappearing behind the ruffled purple curtain.

Cynthia and I were as different as bubble gum and broccoli (except for our ability to get in trouble without much effort). I was a freckle-faced tomboy–skinny and sort of shy, but with enough athletic ability to make most of the clumsy boys my age envious. And on any given day, my copper-red hair looked like I'd spent the entire night twirling around on top of my head.

Cynthia looked like a cherub–pretty and petite, with beautiful blonde curls and a ponytail that was always neatly tied with a shiny satin ribbon. Coordination was not her middle name (board games and jigsaw puzzles were about as physical as she liked to get), but she was always willing, with some coaxing from me, to try just about anything. Even though we'd never be mistaken for twins, we were as close as if we were sisters, and argued like it from time to time.

"Could you walk any slower?" I bellowed when Cynthia finally came ambling across the field chewing on her mitt.

"I'm coming! I'm coming, *Augusta Lee*," she answered, her voice dripping in sarcasm.

"Oh, there's that name," I mumbled under my breath. "She knows I hate it."

I was christened Augusta Lee after my grandfather, Augustus Leopold. But no one dared call me that except my mother, and then only when she was very, very angry, as in "*Augusta Lee! You come in here and pick these dirty clothes up off the floor!*" Cynthia, and anyone else who didn't want a kick in the shins, just called me Gus.

By the time Cynthia moseyed onto the field, the neighborhood kids had already chosen sides. On a good day there were ten of us–five on each team–gathered in the vacant lot where we'd play from early morning until well into the long summer nights.

I stood at home plate, bat on shoulder, impatiently awaiting the pitch as Cynthia meticulously brushed clean a spot on the ground before squatting into the catcher's position. Finally, the game began.

Every now and then one of us would hit one "out of the park," which meant losing another softball in old Mr. Martin's yard. "If I'd wanted kids in my yard I would've had some of my own," he'd yell whenever we'd try to retrieve an errant line drive. Even when he was inside, Daisy, his "lovable" Doberman Pinscher would stand guard. I should add that, to his credit, he'd usually return the balls at the end of the summer, but then the whole process would start over again the next year.

It wasn't an issue this time, because I struck out.

"Nice swing, Gus." Cynthia smirked, flipping the ball back to the pitcher. I just glared and snatched my glove up off the ground. Fortunately for Cynthia, that day we didn't have extra players to cover the outfield, so it was my turn to stop the occasional fly ball from bouncing into the street, or worse yet, into Daisy's slobbering mouth.

The score was tied in the fourth inning when the pitcher's mother abruptly ended the game. "Becky," she called out her back door. "You promised to baby-sit your little sister, remember?" This created a problem since Becky had the only decent bat. However, it wasn't too disappointing since, in spite of what I'd said earlier, I really *was* anxious to hear the new Beatles record. Not only that, Cynthia's house was special.

I lived in a house that only thirty years earlier had been the small barn behind old Mrs. Beanblossom's mansion on the corner. The rooms were barely large enough for furniture, let alone creating mysteries or uncovering secret hiding places. Cynthia, on the other hand, lived in one of those great three-story "exploring houses" that had been in the family for generations. If you came in through the front door (which no one ever did except for Reverend Richert and snooty Mrs.

Fromley, the president of the Ladies Society League), you'd be standing in the foyer. Turning to the left, you could look through French doors into the music room that for some ridiculous reason was off limits to Cynthia and me. The room was brimming with bookcases, all kinds of sheet music from the past forty years or so, and any kind of musical instrument you could possibly think of, most of which came from my family's music store.

The focus of the room was an antique mahogany grand piano that was even older than Cynthia's grandmother, Mama Clara. The only child allowed to actually touch this treasured instrument was Cynthia's older sister, Danielle, who had taken piano lessons for almost ten years and who would play for hours. As we ran through the house we could hear the music of Chopin drifting through the closed doors.

The kitchen, just across the hallway from the den, was small and cozy, and equipped with the most modern appliances. Off to one side in the breakfast nook was a brand new aqua and chrome dinette set where I'd sometimes join Cynthia and her brother and sister for breakfast before school. But what I most looked forward to were the days when I'd walk into the house smelling buttery shortcake baking in the oven, and knowing that as soon as it was done, fresh-picked strawberries and real whipped cream would be piled on top.

On our way up to Cynthia's bedroom that day,

she turned and whispered, "I've got an idea, Gus. Let's get my record player and take it to the den. We can turn it up full blast and see how long it takes for my sister to start screaming!"

"Yeah!" I grinned, taking the stairs two at a time. Danielle was four years older, and had about as much use for us as the Indiana red clay she wiped off her shoes at the front door.

Hurriedly grabbing the record player, we tiptoed back down the stairs, past the music room on our way to the den, being careful not to tip off Danielle. Cynthia headed left into the den, but I turned right, unable to resist the temptation to stick my head in the kitchen and sniff. To my disappointment there were no heavenly aromas coming from the oven.

"C'mon Gus," she ordered, kneeling on the blue plush carpet in the den as she placed the record onto the turntable. "We don't have all day."

I wasn't sure *why* we didn't have all day. I didn't have to be home until supper. Oh well, why argue? Cynthia was boss at her house.

The paneled den on the sunny southeast corner of the house, furnished with a large leather sofa and soft upholstered chairs, always felt warm and comfortable. More than once, I'd curled up in one of those chairs and fallen fast asleep. But not today, because the doors flew open right on cue. "What do you two think you're doing?" Danielle shrieked as she stormed into the room.

Well, that didn't take long–about five seconds,

give or take a second or two.

"Take that irritating music upstairs, and don't come down until I'm through practicing," she yelled, stomping back down the hallway. "I have a recital in three weeks, you know!"

It had only taken one look at her red, angry face to tell us this was no time to argue. We quickly grabbed the records and the record player and ran back upstairs.

"Wow! Did you see her face?" I gasped as soon as we were in the safety of Cynthia's room with the door securely shut.

"Yeah," giggled Cynthia. "My day just isn't complete until I've made her screaming mad at least once."

"I don't know about you," I said, catching my breath, "but in my opinion we should stay out of her way for awhile."

"You're probably right," Cynthia agreed, as we plopped down on her fluffy purple-flowered spread that matched the colors of the iris bed in the side yard.

"So…while we're waiting for Danielle to cool down," she continued, "let's figure out what we're going to do this summer. I do *not* want to be bored out of my skull for the next three months."

The year we both turned twelve had started out with one catastrophe after another. My February birthday party was snowed out by the most ferocious blizzard in almost a hundred years, and the day before her birthday on the first of May, Cynthia got the worst case of chicken pox Dr. Dillard had ever seen. As June approached, however, everything seemed to have settled down. She had a point…it looked like it was going to be just another uneventful summer.

"Well," I stated, "I say we do something that will keep us out of the house. I refuse to spend another vacation being yelled at by your sister and pestered by your stupid brother."

"So, what do you want to do?" she asked.

"Well…we could get the gang together and have a softball tournament," I suggested hopefully.

"No! My leg's still sore from that foul ball you hit today, not to mention the fact that I broke a nail," she snapped, waving her index finger in front of my face and stopping it dead center just inches from the end of my nose.

"Wait, I've got it," she exclaimed.

My eyes uncrossed just in time to see her jump exuberantly off the bed. "Let's investigate the attic! I heard my mother complaining to Dad about how much junk was up there and that they simply *had* to clean it out next week, so I think we should look around up there before they get rid of all the good stuff."

Chapter Two

We'd explored almost every inch of her house, but amazingly the attic was the one place we'd never ventured. After a short discussion and some nervous giggling, Cynthia and I walked across the hallway and stood before the attic door.

Cynthia slowly twisted the knob and the door creaked open, sending a ghostly *whoosh* of cold air down the stairway.

"Uh…maybe this isn't such a great idea," I whispered, peering up into the unknown. I felt as if someone had just slid an icicle down the back of my shirt.

"Oh, Gus! You big coward! Nothing's going to get you. I've been up there hundreds of times. Well, at least three times…maybe…with my dad."

"Well then, why aren't your feet moving?" I sneered, noticing that Cynthia wasn't getting any closer to the first step leading to the attic. But if we were going to find out what exciting and mysterious treasures were up there, one of us had to lead the way.

"C'mon," I sighed.

With Cynthia close on my heels, I silently tiptoed up the wooden stairs, being careful not to disturb anyone or any*thing* that might be waiting to jump out at us from above. A strange feeling came over me as soon as we reached the top, almost as if we'd entered a different world.

"Why's it so warm up here?" I complained, peeling off my favorite Hoosier sweatshirt and tying it around my waist. It was almost June, but that particular afternoon had been cool and damp. Warmth and comfort, however, replaced the coldness we'd felt when we first opened the door. A sunbeam streaming through the window on the opposite side of the attic bounced off the uneven floor, creating a blinding shaft of light in the middle of the room that seemed to shoot straight through the roof.

"It may be warm," acknowledged Cynthia, "but this place gives me the shivers."

"Yeah, me too." I laughed, nervously glancing around. With all the cobwebs hanging from the ceiling, it didn't take much to envision being just one frightful step away from walking into the clutches of a huge Black Widow spider.

Since my imagination was already working overtime, I added much too loudly, "Wouldn't this be a great place for our next Halloween party? No decorating needed!"

Cynthia's look said that *real* spiders and cobwebs had to be about the worst idea for party decorations, but two rusty tricycles that'd been shoved into one corner soon distracted her.   "I haven't seen this thing in years," she answered.

"Bet I can beat you across the attic," I challenged.

"Oh, yeah?" she answered. "Bet you can't!"

After hurriedly brushing off some of the dirt and cobwebs, we jumped on the tiny tricycles and took off across the floor. Knees sticking up under our chins, dodging boxes and pieces of old furniture, we raced in a cloud of dust to an imaginary finish line.

"You're not going to mention this to anyone, are you?" I asked, carefully swinging my long, skinny legs over the handlebars.

"Don't be silly!" Cynthia laughed. "Why would I want anyone to know we've been racing around on these kiddie toys?"

"Speaking of kiddie toys," I snickered, pointing to the far end of the attic, "is that Little Cynthia's baby carriage?"

Cynthia gave me *the look* and huffed, "I'd be careful if I were you, Gus. My mom has pictures of the two of us sitting in that carriage, and believe me, you do *not* want me passing them around at school next fall."

Opening my mouth to say something really smart, I decided this might be one time to keep it shut. I had this image of sitting in the carriage with my silly-looking baby face, the little tufts of red hair adorning the top of my head, as I mugged an idiotic, toothless grin for the camera.

While I casually turned to continue searching

the attic, Cynthia's tone softened as she looked at the carriage and laughed, "Yeah, Mother said we used to sit in there and 'talk' for hours."

"We still do," I added cheerfully, "but I think we've outgrown the carriage by a few years."

After opening boxes and doing some basic snooping around, we were just about to give up finding anything exciting when Cynthia said quietly, "Look at that, Gus."

Behind a dense curtain of cobwebs...behind an antique table and lamp...behind a stack of faded suitcases...appeared the top of a huge, dust-covered old trunk. After carefully moving a hand-blown glass lamp without breaking it, and dragging the antique table to one side, we pushed the suitcases away and there it was–the biggest trunk I'd ever seen! Bigger than my grandma's old steamer trunk.

"You don't suppose it's really a coffin with a body in it, do you?" I whispered, wide-eyed.

"Are you nuts?" She laughed. "That's crazy, even for you, Gus. Besides, don't you think a dead body would smell in this heat?"

"Yeah," I laughed sheepishly. "Guess I just got caught up in the moment...you know, with the spiders and cobwebs and all."

"Well...do you wanna see what's *really* in it?" she asked expectantly.

"Yeah...okay," I said, determined to run like heck if a zombie jumped out!

Cynthia and I knelt down in front of the trunk

and tried to lift the lid.

"Man! This is heavy," I groaned, struggling to lift one side while Cynthia pulled with all her might on the other. Finally the rusty hinges gave way and the lid slowly creaked open.

Peeking inside, we saw that it was filled with all kinds of old clothes, hats, and…

"*Eeeeeekkk*!" I leaped to my feet. "It's *alive*!"

I was halfway down the stairs when I heard, "You mean this old *fur*?" Cynthia snickered, dangling it in the air. "I don't think it's been alive for several years, Gus."

Feeling silly, I walked slowly up the steps and across the attic floor to the trunk, only to have Cynthia shove the old thing right in my face. "Here, Gus! Be careful! It might bite and give you rabies!"

"Ah...*choo*! Ah…ah…*choo!*" I sneezed over and over and over from the dust flying off the fur.

"Stop it, Gus," Cynthia said disgustedly. "You're blowing boogers all over everything!"

"Well, excu-u-u-use me, but this stuff smells moldy! I'll bet no one's been in this trunk for a hundred years!" As my sneezing fit started winding down, I noticed Cynthia peering into the trunk at a dress that was neatly folded on top. She pulled out a faded ballerina costume and shook dust everywhere.

Oh, oh, here I go again! "Ah…ah…*ah*…*CHOO*!" Fortunately, she was too busy admiring the dress to yell at me again. After dabbing tears from the corners of my eyes with the tail of my rumpled shirt, I noticed the costume was a light pink with tarnished gold braiding around the neck. Next, Cynthia pulled out a pair of ballet shoes that appeared to have tiny pieces of dull glass glued on them. "This outfit is too big to be mine," she said, holding up the dress, "and I'm sure it doesn't belong to Danielle because no one would dare drag her away from her precious piano long enough to take dancing lessons."

"Well, one thing's sure," I said, "even as dirty as this dress is, it still looks like nothing a mere mortal would wear, but more like something belonging to a fairy princess."

I guess the image of looking like a princess was far too much for Cynthia to resist, because she quickly put on the costume and slipped into the ballet shoes.

"Where's a mirror when you need one?" she said, stomping her foot in frustration.

I didn't need a mirror to see how silly she looked in the dress. It was hanging nearly to the floor, especially since Cynthia was a couple of inches shorter than most girls our age. But in spite of that– like magic–she began *dancing*! Not like the Cynthia I'd seen stumble more than once during the ballet lessons our mothers had insisted we take for over three years, and not the Cynthia who'd fallen awkwardly off the stage during our last recital. *This*

Cynthia danced across the floor, leaping high into the air with the grace of a prima ballerina.

"Wow," I said with a little envy in my voice, "I've never seen you dance like that at our ballet lessons!"

"Well, you weren't the most elegant dancer in class either," she said, still twirling around the room.

She had me there, but I still couldn't believe she managed to stay on her feet.

The envy and the questions soon disappeared when she finally stopped leaping about the room, took off the dress, and tripped while slipping out of the ballet shoes. We both laughed, probably more from relief, because everything seemed to be back to normal with Cynthia's return to her old clumsy self.

"Well, that was kinda weird," I said quietly, as we made our way back down the stairs. We laughed, but I noticed we were both strangely quiet and didn't mention Cynthia's newfound "talent" for the rest of the day. Instead, we just went back to playing the games that twelve-year-old girls usually play, and didn't talk about the attic for the rest of the week.

I don't know what made us decide to go back up to the attic. Maybe curiosity, maybe boredom— probably a little of both. When we climbed the stairs and stepped into the attic the second time, things seemed a little different. For instance, looking down at the floor I noticed the dusty footprints we'd made previously had disappeared. It was almost as if we hadn't been there at all because the tricycles were once again back where we found them, covered with cobwebs, just like before. The air, which had been so warm and inviting, was now very cold and still, even though summer had finally arrived and the day was hot and muggy. I started getting the creepy feeling that we should turn around and go right back down the stairs, but after the "fur incident," I didn't want to act scared. How different that day, and our lives, might have been if I'd only known how scared Cynthia was, because then we would've missed out on the greatest adventure of our lives.

Chapter Three

I was just getting ready to grab Cynthia and get out of the attic as fast as possible when I found us being pulled like magnets across the floor. Standing before the trunk, without knowing exactly how we got there, Cynthia stammered, "Gus…it…looks different, doesn't it?"

"Yeah," I answered slowly. "It looks…brand new! Where's all the dust? Even the rust and the scratches are gone! Remember how dull the latch and the hinges were? Now they look like someone just polished them!"

"That same someone must be trying to play tricks on us," she said looking around suspiciously. "But who…or *what*…could it be?"

We slowly opened the lid to the trunk, which this time was as light as a feather, and were relieved to see that the clothes were still there, and that nothing was moving.

"Notice anything different…about the ballet dress?" I asked hesitantly.

"Uh huh," she said, slowly running her hand across the soft, silky fabric. "It's clean and doesn't smell musty like before."

"Have you also noticed I'm not sneezing my fool

head off?" I said, gratefully.

Cynthia was too busy holding up the costume to answer, but I saw that it was now a bright rose-colored pink, and the braiding around the neck was as shiny as 24-carat gold. The dull glass that had been glued onto the ballet slippers had been replaced with shimmering rhinestones.

Pulling the costume out of the trunk, she pointed at something that had been lying underneath. "Look at this old-fashioned sailor dress! I didn't see it before, did you?"

I picked the dress out of the trunk and held it up to me. It looked like new and was a brilliant navy blue with white braiding around the collar and sleeves. Although I was plenty tall for the dress, I could tell it would hang like a limp dishrag on my skinny frame.

"It's just my size," I said sarcastically, knowing I would have to magically gain ten pounds or so before the dress would come close to fitting.

"Hey, Gus," Cynthia exclaimed, paying no attention to me as she rooted through the trunk. "I found a matching sailor hat and a pair of patent leather shoes. Oh, you just have to try them on."

"Gee," I said, turning to Cynthia. "What surprise will this dress have for me since the ballet costume turned you into a graceful dancer?"

As I daydreamed about being a wealthy passenger on a large oceangoing vessel, to my horror the image changed and I saw myself becoming violently seasick over the railing. Maybe a cruise wasn't such a great idea since I get queasy just riding in the car.

But I just shrugged. "Guess it couldn't hurt to try on the dress and see what happens."

Shivering from either anticipation or the cold, I wasn't sure which, I slipped the dress over my head. Nothing happened. Then I slipped on the shoes. Nothing happened. I put on the hat and turned, expecting to hear Cynthia tell me how silly I looked when, with no warning at all, I was lifted off the floor and pulled swiftly into the trunk. The last thing I saw was Cynthia's horrified face.

I felt like a flying brick–heavy, but almost weightless at the same time. I was moving very rapidly in complete darkness, then in radiant light. The sun was out. No, it was the moon and the stars! *This is amazing! How can I be traveling this fast without a hint of motion sickness?* In an instant I found myself passing through the most beautiful bright green and purple colors I'd ever seen. They reminded me of one night a few years back when, through some freak of nature, our small Southern Indiana town was blessed with the Northern Lights– a show that was usually reserved for Minnesota or Maine. Then, just as abruptly as I began my strange trip, I stopped moving and felt as if I'd been suspended in some strange, unknown universe.

I'm not sure if minutes or hours had passed before I saw a bright flash of light and found myself standing in the middle of Cynthia's kitchen. At least it looked at first glance like Cynthia's kitchen, but I soon realized everything in the room was different.

The first thing that looked out of place was an old cast iron kettle boiling on the stove...a *wood* stove no less! Then I sensed the smell of bread baking in the oven, which reminded me that Cynthia and I had skipped lunch. Speaking of food, the new, shiny chrome dinette set was gone, replaced by a wooden table that was set with the old, antique dishes that Cynthia's mother kept for special occasions. The kitchen sink no longer had faucets...it had a pump! And where did this old ice chest come from? Just the other day, Cynthia was showing off their brand new Kelvinator with its own ice cube trays, swing-out egg holders, and juice bar right inside the door! I remember hearing my mom say, enviously, that it must've "set them back a pretty penny."

I stepped through the kitchen door into the hallway, where a colorful rag rug adorned the rich wooden floor. "I must be going crazy," I said to myself. "This floor was turquoise and black linoleum the last time I ran through here!"

Peeking into the family room, nothing was as I remembered. How could everything change in the blink of an eye? Two uncomfortable-looking wooden rockers replaced the snuggly, overstuffed chairs on either side of the fireplace, and a scratchy-looking brown upholstered sofa sat on the far side of the room underneath the double windows.

I wandered down the hallway toward the music room, which, thankfully, looked very much the same. The grand piano still sat majestically in one corner, the candelabra still gracing the matching mahogany end table beside the heavily draped window facing Oak Street. I took a comforting glance around before continuing my tour.

As I turned to go up the stairs, however, I heard, "Clara? Is that you?"

Spinning around in the direction of the voice, I saw a tall, blond-haired, apron-clad woman walk from the kitchen into the hallway.

"Oh, hello, Bess," the stern-looking woman said, sounding somewhat annoyed. "Will you tell Clara it's almost time to eat?"

Tell Clara *what*? Why is she calling me Bess? And who the heck is she anyway? I've never seen her before in my life because...believe me, I'd remember this old grump. No, wait...I *have* seen her somewhere, I just don't know where. The only Bess I know is my grandmother, and I've always fondly called Cynthia's grandmother Mama Clara. Now, why in the world would this woman mistake me for my grandmother?

All of a sudden it hit me. I knew where I'd seen her! In *pictures!* She was Cynthia's *great-grandmother!* Oh, this was getting way too strange...I had to get out of there, and fast!

But before I could move, she asked sharply,

"Bess? Isn't that Clara's new dress you're wearing? Maybe you should take it off, dear, even though it does fit you very nicely. She needs to wear it to school tomorrow."

Is she nuts? This baggy thing fits me nicely? Well, anyway, she didn't have to tell me twice.

"Uh…sure. I'll take it off right now," I said, my voice almost squeaking with fright.

The woman cocked her head and looked puzzled as if she wanted to question me some more, but I wasn't going to hang around until she figured out I wasn't Bess. She had her mouth open to speak, but I quickly made my escape up the stairway to the second floor.

My instincts said to run for the attic, so I threw open the door and bounded up the stairs as fast as I could, hoping to find a way to escape from this very weird dream.

My heart sank. Nothing looked the same up here either. I practically stumbled over a small wooden cradle, and Cynthia's baby carriage was gone. The tricycles were missing too. There was a large, strange-looking three-wheeled bicycle in the corner that didn't look like it had been ridden for a while because one of the back wheels had fallen off and was lying on the floor. *Too bad*, I thought miserably, *I might need some transportation out of here*. As I turned to make my way back downstairs, I spotted it. What a relief! Although the contents of the attic were nothing like the one I had abruptly left, the trunk was still there sitting behind an old marble-top table, thank goodness. Now, to figure out whether this was a "round trip" or just "one way," I opened the trunk and proceeded to dive in headfirst.

"*Ow*! That hurt!" Besides that, it didn't work– I'm still here, with my head in the trunk and my feet sticking straight up in the air. Pulling myself out, and beginning to fear I was going to be trapped forever in the past with Cynthia's grouchy great-grandmother, I noticed the sailor hat lying beside the trunk. I reached down, snatched it off the floor, and put it on my head.

Zoom! I was taking the same trip as before, only in reverse.

Chapter Four

In an instant I was standing, somewhat stunned, back in the attic I'd unexpectedly departed, and staring at a bug-eyed, babbling Cynthia.

She couldn't speak for several seconds, then finally stammered, "Wh–wh–where did you go?"

What in the world was I supposed to tell her? "How the heck should *I* know?" I snapped, feeling bewildered as I stood there rubbing the very real bump on my head.

Since I didn't have the foggiest idea, how was I supposed to tell *her*? I knew she deserved some kind of explanation, but how could I possibly explain what I *think* had just happened? Guess I'll just have to blurt it out.

"Cynthia...uh...you're not gonna believe this, but I just had a conversation with...your...uh, great-grandmother...in your kitchen!"

Even though she'd just witnessed my disappearance into a trunk full of clothes, I could tell she thought I'd lost my mind.

"Gus, do you really expect me to believe you just talked to my great-grandmother, Nana Anna?" She sighed. "She's only been dead for twenty years!"

"Well…yeah, I know it sounds pretty ridiculous." I chuckled nervously as I struggled to make sense of my trip and also grasp the silliness of someone actually being called "Nana Anna."

In spite of Cynthia's skepticism, I began spilling out the whole story of traveling through the strange bright lights and ending up in what I first thought was Cynthia's kitchen. How all the kitchen appliances and furniture had changed, smelling the bread baking in that antique oven, how all the furniture had changed in the den, being called Bess, and being told to call Clara for lunch.

"I could tell I was going to get into trouble with your Nana Anna if I didn't take off the dress," I said, "but I kept wondering why she was calling me Bess. Have you heard any stories about your great-grandmother having extremely bad eyesight?"

"No. I don't even think she wore glasses," Cynthia answered, her eyes narrowing in thought, "Ya know, Gus, you do look a little like pictures I've seen of your grandmother when she was about our age, but I'd imagine anyone could tell you apart."

"Well, that's what I thought." I sniffed. "But anyway, she looked like she was in a bad mood and getting more suspicious by the minute, so I ran to the attic as fast as I could hoping I'd find my way back here…and it worked!"

"I can remember Mama Clara saying that Nana Anna wasn't a happy person, although she never said why. Besides, how did you have so much time to spend with my great-grandmother when you were only gone a few seconds?" she questioned.

"A few seconds? But...but...I'm telling the truth!" I could tell by the cynical look on her face it was going to take more than this wild story to convince her.

"I don't know how long I was there, but *I was there*," I insisted. "You'll just have to come back with me and see for yourself!"

Did I just say that? How could I even *consider* taking that crazy trip again? I'm not sure where I'd been or how lucky I was to get back, I just knew, deep down, that with all the experiences Cynthia and I had shared over the years, this was something I couldn't keep to myself. Since I was pretty sure my ability to "fly" through the trunk had something to do with Clara's dress, I suggested that Cynthia put it on to see if it worked for her.

"Oh, no, Gus," she said, shaking her head and backing away from the trunk...and me. "If you really took some wild ride through that thing, I'm not going. What if I couldn't get back? What if I got stuck floating forever in those crazy, bright lights you traveled through?"

"I promise you won't," I insisted, wondering how I could possibly convince her since I wasn't convinced myself.

She reached hesitantly for the dress, then stopped, crossed her arms, and said firmly, "Gus, I'm not going to do this unless you promise you'll be right behind me."

"Cross my heart and hope to die," I swore, sincerely hoping it wouldn't come to that.

As soon as we started tearing through the trunk looking for another dress that might be suitable for travel, I pictured Cynthia being magically transformed into an accomplished ballet dancer. Hmmm…

"That's it! I'll bet you can use the ballet costume," I shouted. "I just know it'll work. Maybe the reason you weren't sucked into the trunk the first time you had the dress on was because it wasn't 'magically' prepared for travel."

It sounded pretty silly when I said it out loud, and I couldn't blame Cynthia for looking at me as if I'd left my brains in the trunk.

"Gus, you're just making me more nervous, not to mention starting to sound *really* weird," she said impatiently as she pulled on the dress, slipped into the ballet shoes, then stood anxiously in front of the trunk. I told her to clear her mind and think about diving into the trunk. She took a deep breath, flew in headfirst, and accomplished nothing more than looking as ridiculous as I must've looked, upside down in that gigantic trunk with those pink slippers waving frantically in the air. As I pulled her out, I noticed she had some kind of flower-covered tiara hanging on her wrist. It had the same gold braiding and several shades of pink roses that matched the ballet dress she was wearing.

"Where did this come from?" She slowly placed the tiara on her head, turned to me, and asked, "Do you think this goes with the dress?" But before I answered, she was gone. It *worked*! I stood motionless for a moment. Then, remembering my promise to Cynthia, I quickly slipped my sailor hat back on my head, and away I went, silently praying we'd both end up in the same place.

Chapter Five

Once again I was standing in the old kitchen, but Cynthia was nowhere in sight.

Oh, this isn't good at all. What if she's gotten stuck in some Never-Never Land, and I'd never see her again? I got her into this, and now my best friend may be gone forever. As I was feeling all the doom and despair my twelve-year-old brain could handle, I heard an angry voice coming from upstairs.

"Clara! How many times have I told you not to play in that ballet dress?" I listened for a reply, but all I could make out were the sounds of faint stammering. That settles it. If Nana Anna is yelling at Cynthia and calling her Clara, then she definitely needs glasses. I'd better get up there fast.

As I reached the second-floor landing, I saw a very bewildered Cynthia standing at the doorway to her room—or I guess in this case it was Clara's room—staring in total disbelief at the same tall, blonde-haired woman I'd seen on my earlier trip—her great-grandmother, Nana Anna. I'm sure Cynthia now understood why I was so anxious to get away from this frightening woman.

I decided to steer clear of this conversation since

I was still in Clara's school dress and didn't want to get yelled at for not taking it off, as I'd been ordered. Sneaking back down a couple of stairs, I peeked over the banister at my friend's face, wondering if she'd ever be able to speak again.

"I'm sorry, M…M…Ma'am," Cynthia finally managed to say.

"Well, you should be, Clara. First you lose Belle's gold locket, and now it seems you're determined to ruin the last memory we have of her," Clara's mother snapped. "You'll just have to be punished."

Oh, oh, this was getting serious. I could tell Cynthia had no idea what Nana Anna was talking about, and wasn't enjoying the idea of taking the blame for something that must've happened two generations before she was even born. I quickly decided I'd have to create a diversion. Stumbling back up the stairs past Cynthia and Nana Anna, and mumbling something about being sorry I was still wearing Clara's dress, I ran into the bedroom. Thank goodness it worked. Nana Anna heaved a sigh, threw up her hands in frustration, and went back downstairs to the kitchen.

"Well, genius," Cynthia said sarcastically as she shut Clara's bedroom door, "now that I've gotten yelled at by my *dead* great-grandmother, any other trips you want to take?"

"Hey, you're forgetting that I got yelled at too," I snapped. "All I'm sure of at this point in time is that your Nana Anna's personality isn't anything like her sweet-sounding name, and in her foul mood I don't want to be caught in Clara's dress again."

"Stop blaming me for my great-grandmother's rotten personality." Cynthia plopped down on the white chenille bedspread and pouted. I ignored her and tried to figure out if we should go back or do some investigating, although I wasn't sure Cynthia would be any help at all.

While my mind went back and forth between being brave and adventurous, and wanting to get back to the security of our own homes, Cynthia finally spoke, "You know, I didn't think it was possible, but Mama Clara and your Grandma Bess must've gotten into more trouble in their day than *we* do in ours! I don't know about you, Gus, but I don't like this place one bit!"

She got no argument from me. It was decided that we'd had enough adventuring for the moment, so we tiptoed back up to the attic and were sucked through the trunk. In the bat of an eye we found ourselves in the familiar surroundings of Cynthia's attic.

Storing the ballerina costume and the sailor dress in the trunk, we slipped down the attic stairs and into the security of Cynthia's bedroom. It appeared that very little time had passed, and that we hadn't been missed.

"Wow! What a cool trip," Cynthia said as she did an awkward swan dive onto her bed.

I didn't know whether to laugh or scream, since just minutes earlier she'd been tongue-tied and terrified while staring into the angry face of her great-grandmother. Fortunately for Cynthia, I was speechless.

"I'm still confused about why Nana Anna thought you were Bess and I was Clara." Cynthia shook her head in bewilderment. "I resemble pictures I've seen of Mama Clara as a girl, just like you and your Grandma Bess, but anyone should be able to tell the difference."

"And not only that," I added, "if we were really back in the olden days of our grandmothers, then where were the real Clara and Bess?"

Cynthia shrugged her shoulders and I decided to stop wasting time trying to figure it out since anything would have been just a guess at that point, and my head was starting to hurt. Besides, we had more important things to talk about, such as if and when we were going back.

"Do you think we could find out anything from Mama Clara?" Cynthia asked. "Do you think she'd remember about the locket or Great-Aunt Isabelle's ballet dress? Maybe she'll know if the family ever heard from her. I know her memory isn't what it used to be, but she usually just forgets things like what she had for lunch. I can remember hearing her tell hundreds of stories about her childhood and what it was like growing up in this house. I've even heard her brag about how hers was the first house in town to have indoor plumbing."

As I sat there contemplating the inconvenience of outdoor plumbing, Cynthia jumped up, "Let's go visit Mama Clara and see if we can smooth-talk her into telling us some stories about the old days."

Chapter Six

Mama Clara wasn't one of those "cookie baking" grandmas. She'd been a businesswoman, helping her husband and then her son run the family clothing store. It was unusual in those days for a wife and mother to also work outside the home, but she had managed to do both quite well. We never missed the cookies because she always made time for us.

When Cynthia's grandfather died ten years earlier, Mama Clara moved into the small cottage next to the family home. I loved playing there because she didn't have toys–she let us play with her stuff! We had elegant tea parties with her white, daisy-covered dishes and bright yellow cups and saucers. We were allowed to dress up in her clothes and high heels, and accessorize with her fancy earrings and long strands of multicolored beads…adding the finishing touch with an all-too-generous spray of exotic perfume.

We burst in the door just as Mama Clara was walking out of her quaint little kitchen dressed in one of her starched, paisley print dresses that she wore whether she was going out or staying in. "What are you girls up to?" she asked suspiciously, settling into her rocking chair while carefully balancing her afternoon cup of Earl Grey tea. Her silvery-blonde hair was, as usual, pinned in a neat little bun on top of her head. She looked a little frail sitting in that oversized chair, but the twinkle in her watchful eyes never seemed to dim. "I can tell you two have something on your minds," she observed.

How did she know we were up to something? "Oh, nothing special, Mama Clara," Cynthia lied, glancing at me out of the corner of her eye just as Mama Clara took a sip of tea. "We were…uh…hoping you'd tell us a couple of stories about when you were a little girl. We have to do a report for school on our family history," she said, getting in deeper and deeper, "and I know you're the oldest…uh, I mean you know more about our family history than anyone else."

Mama Clara laughed, and told Cynthia she was right the first time. "I am the oldest, dear, and I have as many family stories to tell as you have time to hear. Now, is there any particular place you want me to start?"

"A story about Aunt Isabelle," I shouted.

Cynthia jabbed me with a painful elbow to the ribs. Guess that was a little too obvious since we don't want anyone, even Mama Clara, to become suspicious of our attic activities of the past few weeks.

But Mama Clara didn't seem to notice my outburst, or Cynthia poking me for that matter, because she was deep in thought. "*Ahhh*…Aunt Belle," she sighed. "Well, actually, Cynthia, she was my aunt, and your great-great aunt, but I haven't thought of her in so many years. I didn't really know her because, from what I've been told, she spent her life in France. However, I used to sit for hours and listen to my mother tell stories about her."

Mama Clara settled back in her chair and continued, "Nana Anna, who was my mother and your great-grandmother, came to America with her mother and father when she was eighteen, but her sister Isabelle, who was two years older, stayed behind in Paris. She was on her way to becoming an accomplished dancer and couldn't bear the thought of giving it up."

Cynthia and I looked wide-eyed at each other and said in unison, "A *dancer*? What *kind* of dancer?"

"Why, she was a ballerina," Mama Clara answered. "And one of the finest until her destiny unexpectedly changed." All at once we noticed a very sad, faraway look in her eyes.

Realizing it was crucial to keep her on the subject or we'd never find out anything about Isabelle and the locket, Cynthia persisted, "Mama Clara, Mama Clara! Why did Isabelle quit dancing?"

Mama Clara snapped back to the present and said that Belle's last letter to her sister said that she'd met the most perfect man in Paris and was getting married soon. To the surprise of Anna and the rest of the family, Belle had decided to give up her dream to become a prima ballerina so she could concentrate on becoming a good wife and eventually a mother. It seemed there was no way that dancing would fit into her new life. Along with the letter was a package containing Belle's favorite ballerina costume and a gold locket. She wanted Anna to keep the locket and the costume so she'd always remember Belle and the fun they had growing up together.

"That was the last time anyone in the family heard from her. Nana Anna wrote letters to her almost every week, but they all came back unopened. Several months later we found out that Belle's 'perfect man' had apparently walked out on her just days before the wedding and, soon after he left, she too disappeared," Mama Clara said.

"Come to think of it, not long after we received Belle's package, Nana Anna mailed a steamship ticket to her hoping she would visit the family in America, but it was sent back with a letter from her former landlady saying that she'd moved. No one ever found out what happened to her."

"So, what became of the locket? What did it look like? Do you still have it?" I asked eagerly.

"Sadly, no," she said. "I lost it many, many years ago, and I don't think my mother ever quite forgave me. I can still remember, though, how that gold, bell-shaped locket felt around my neck. On the outside was engraved the initial 'B,' but what made the locket even more special were the pictures inside." She paused for a moment.

"What pictures?" Cynthia and I persisted in unison.

Mama Clara chuckled and said, "Well, I'm glad to see you really are listening. There were pictures in the locket of the two sisters, Isabelle and Anna," she continued. "As I remember, they were taken just before Mother and the rest of the family left for America, leaving Isabelle in Paris. Come to think of it, Cynthia, you look just like I picture Aunt Belle looked at your age—her hair was a little darker, but you have the same heart-shaped face, deep blue eyes, and sunny smile. Well, anyway, you can imagine how much trouble I got into when I lost the locket."

Cynthia and I glanced at each other. Oh, we could more than imagine—we saw for ourselves just how much trouble she got into.

She went on to say that my grandmother, Bess, found out about the locket one day when she was playing at the house, and had insisted on seeing it. Clara knew she wasn't supposed to touch it, but with Bess's curiosity and Clara's desire to show off the locket, she went against her better judgment. The two girls sneaked into Nana Anna's room, took the locket out of the special ribbon-tied box, and then scurried up the attic stairs.

"Neither one of us had ever seen a more beautiful piece of jewelry," Mama Clara exclaimed. "We both took turns trying it on and admiring how elegant we looked with the bell-shaped locket around our necks, along with furs draped over our shoulders that we'd dug out of an old trunk, which is probably why we didn't hear Nana Anna open the attic door and walk up the steps. I knew I didn't want to get caught with the locket so I quickly threw it, and the fur I was wearing, into the trunk thinking I could sneak back later that night and retrieve it."

"You weren't able to find it?" Cynthia asked.

Mama Clara shook her head, "I went back up after dinner and searched the trunk for as long as I could without being missed, and then Bess and I went back up the next day and looked again. We took everything out of that trunk, piece by piece, but it had disappeared. Not long after that, the attic was cleaned, the junk was tossed out, and some of the old clothes were given away. I don't know if the locket was accidentally thrown away, but I had a terrible feeling I'd never see it again, and finally had to admit to my mother I'd disobeyed her and lost her most prized possession."

Mama Clara said sadly, "A few weeks later, Mother folded the beautiful ballet dress, and placed it in that same trunk in the attic. She just couldn't bear to look at it again, and neither could I. To this day, I still haven't opened that trunk."

Cynthia and I were speechless for the first time

in our young lives. We didn't know why, but we both felt that with our discovery of the magic trunk, we had somehow been drawn into solving a fifty-year-old mystery about the dress, the locket, and the disappearance of Isabelle.

Barely able to contain ourselves, we ran back to Cynthia's house and into the privacy of her bedroom.

"Can you believe this?" I whispered, just in case Cynthia's pesky brother was listening at the door. "We were actually there when Nana Anna thought she was scolding Mama Clara about losing the locket. That must've really happened!"

"Yeah," Cynthia said. "And I think Mama Clara is just as sad today as she was the day she lost it. I sure wish there was something we could do for her."

"Maybe we could go back and find it," I said, almost hoping that Cynthia would think the idea was as ridiculous as I did.

But I could tell by the eager look on her face that she thought this was the greatest idea I'd had in all my twelve years.

"Yeah," she said, excitedly. "All we have to figure out is how to explore Mama Clara's home without getting in trouble for wearing Isabelle's ballet dress and Clara's good school dress."

"How about this?" I suggested, resigned to the fact that we were going to be making another trip despite the possibility of another confrontation with Nana Anna. "When we go back through the trunk, why don't you slip into Clara's room and change into one of her old outfits. Then we can sneak out of the house and go to my Grandmother Bess's house."

Cynthia screwed up her face and asked, "Why would we do that?"

"Because," I said impatiently, eager to continue telling my plan, "we can figure out how to slip into her house, find her bedroom, and borrow one of her dresses."

Cynthia looked a little doubtful at this point, but finally agreed. "Well, it might work. But what do we do if we just happen to run into our grandmothers while we're rummaging through their clothes?" she smugly asked.

"I don't know." I shrugged, and then started moving like I was beginning an embarrassingly awkward hula. "Maybe we can start swaying back and forth, waving our arms like ghosts and they'll think they're having a nightmare."

Cynthia shook her head and sighed, "Sometimes you scare me, Gus."

She's not alone. Sometimes I scare myself.

But before we could think of any more reasons to try and forget Mama Clara's sadness over losing Aunt Belle's locket so many years ago, we ran back to the attic and put on the ballet costume and the sailor dress for another journey into the past. There was no indication we'd have any luck finding the locket, but we knew we had to try for Mama Clara's sake–wanting more than anything to pay her back for all the love and kindness she'd given us in our twelve short years.

Chapter Seven

Traveling back in time through the trunk found us once more in Clara's attic. Cautiously making our way down the stairs, we listened at the door to make sure no one was wandering around on the second floor. Sneaking into Clara's bedroom, Cynthia changed into a long, rather shapeless, faded brown dress she found lying on the bed, and a pair of Clara's black high-button shoes.

"Well, Nana Anna surely can't get upset if I wear *this* old thing," she said disgustedly.

I wanted to laugh, but kept it to myself since I had no idea what kind of "fashion statement" I'd find in Bess's wardrobe.

We left the house without being seen and started on our way to my grandmother's house, amazed at all the horse-drawn buggies making their way along the dirt streets around the town square. Even though there were a few "horseless carriages" speeding around town at about ten miles per hour, I guess they hadn't really caught on yet. At least getting run over by one wasn't a big concern.

Right in the middle of the town square sat the first state capitol of Indiana. Much history had been made in the old limestone building, which served the state for twelve years in the early 1800s until it was decided to move it to a more central location–Indianapolis. According to my Indiana history classes, the late June summer had made the building so oppressive that the state constitution was approved under the shading branches of a monstrous elm tree…which gave me an idea.

"C'mon. Up this street."

"Where are we going?" Cynthia whined. "This isn't the way to your grandmother's."

"No," I said slyly, "but there's something I want to see."

I walked quickly up the steep, tree-lined street as Cynthia plodded grudgingly behind. I turned the corner expectantly, and there it was–in all its majesty–the Constitutional Elm.

"Wow." I stopped abruptly as Cynthia plowed into the back of me.

"Ow! What's wrong with you, Gus?" Then she gasped. That old tree had been nothing but a petrified stump since Dutch elm disease killed it in 1925. Now its full, leaf-covered branches spread out 100 feet, even shading the other side of the street.

"Can you believe it?" I said, awestruck.

Cynthia was somewhat less impressed. "Sure, sure, it's great. Now can we get back to the original plan? Your grandmother's house?" she said impatiently.

I was amazed. Right in front of us was probably

the best climbing tree in the whole county, and she wanted to leave. "But, Cynthia," I pleaded, "look at these branches. I'll bet we could see the whole town from the top!"

"You have lost your mind, Gus. That tree has to be three stories high. If you think I'm going to risk breaking my neck, you're insane." She shook her head and stomped back down the sidewalk toward town, obviously appalled at my suggestion.

I stood there for a minute, taking in the magnificent tree, the history, and most of all, the lost opportunity to scale those great limbs.

Pouting all the way down the street, my mood soon lifted as a familiar landmark came into view.

"Hey," I shouted as we neared a bright green storefront with a monstrous strawberry ice cream cone painted on the window. "My dad used to tell me stories about Rosenbarger's Ice Cream Emporium and how he'd look forward to the days when he could scrape together fifteen cents for a frosted malt." I longingly sighed, "Sure wish I'd thought to bring some money with me," as we passed a couple of kids walking casually down the street eating their sundaes.

"Gus," Cynthia snapped. "We have more important things to think about than that bottomless pit you call a stomach."

I knew she was right, so I didn't argue *this* time.

Our stroll through town also took us past the train station, although it's hard to use the word "train" without laughing since it consisted of an engine, one passenger car, and a caboose. The Lizzie Lou, as it was called–named after the station owner's two daughters, Elizabeth and Louisa–took passengers or valuable cargo the amazing distance of fifteen miles north to the next small town and back again. Despite its lack of length, however, it would years later become one of the town's main tourist attractions, and still be called the Lizzie Lou.

We passed the Dream Theatre that would be showing movies fifty years in the future until it burned to the ground in one of the most spectacular fires the town had ever seen. I felt as if I'd walked back into one of the old family photographs that I now wish I'd paid more attention to, because I'd forgotten which Mill Street house was my grandmother's.

As if reading my mind, Cynthia asked, "Okay, Gus, which one is it?"

"Er…uh…I think it's this one…no, it's that one." I pointed, not having a clue which one it was. Everything looked so different in my grandmother's day from the way it looked in mine.

About the time I was ready to admit to Cynthia I wasn't really sure, a huge tan and white collie came bounding down from the hill above us. We were trying to decide whether to run or just freeze in our tracks when he headed straight for me, jumped up, and knocked me flat on the ground.

"Biff," I yelled without thinking, "get *off* me!" I

must've guessed right because he let me up and then stood there wagging his tail and whining as if his best friend had just returned from a long journey.

"How in the world did you know his name?" Cynthia asked.

"I don't know," I said hesitantly. "I remember seeing pictures of a collie named Biff in one of my grandmother's photo albums, and he sure looks the same. Besides, he seems to like it."

"I think he came from that house on top of the hill," observed Cynthia.

Glancing up, I shouted, "That's it! I remember now! On one of our walks a couple of years ago, my grandmother pointed out that white house on the hill with the porch that wraps all the way around the front." *Thank goodness for good ol' Biff,* I sighed to myself.

Guided by the rambunctious collie, we made our way up the steep dirt path that led to the front porch. I almost made the mistake of knocking on the front door, but caught myself just in time as I realized I probably should act like this is my house. Maybe, if we were lucky, we could sneak in, get what we needed, then sneak out without being seen. I hesitantly opened the door, and Cynthia and I tiptoed into the hallway of my Grandma Bess's home.

As I gazed around, trying to decide where to go next, I heard a stern voice call, "Bess? Come in here, please." Oh, no. That sounded like *more* trouble! Now what had my grandmother done that I'm going to get blamed for?

Thanks to a big shove from behind by Cynthia, I went stumbling into the living room, although I think they called them "parlors" back then. Keeping my head down so she wouldn't get a good look at my face, I tried to sneak a peek at the lady in front of me. I was going to have to be a little careful because I never saw any pictures of my great-grandmother. The only thing I remembered from Grandma Bess's stories was that she called her "Mama." As I stood there shifting from one foot to the other, Cynthia–the coward–stayed in the hallway just out of sight.

"Bess, did you remember to wipe your feet before coming into the house?" this petite, dark-haired woman asked, never looking up from her embroidery.

I immediately turned and looked over my left shoulder at the floor. "Uh...no, ma'am," I answered, seeing the trail of mud I'd left behind.

"Bess, what am I going to do with you? Sometimes I just can't believe you're my daughter," she said staring straight at me with exasperation written all over her face. "I always try to keep a nice clean house, and you're always coming along right behind me getting it dirty again! When will you ever learn?"

Well, this was certainly a new experience in my life–getting blamed for years of muddy footprints left by my grandmother. At least I got the information I was looking for–my great-grandmother, Marie Julia, was scolding me.

I kept my head down as far as possible to hide my face while mumbling, "I'm sorry, Mama. It won't happen again."

Guess I wasn't in too much trouble because she broke into a smile and asked cheerfully, "Is that Clara with you?" As I turned in the direction of the hallway, I saw Cynthia peek around the corner with a stupid grin on her face. "You can stay for dinner, dear, if it's all right with your mother. We'll be sitting down to eat, Bess, as soon as your father arrives, so please don't wander off."

I almost choked at that statement. *Wander off!* What would she think if she knew we'd already *wandered off* about fifty years!

"No, Mama. We'll be here," I said eagerly, wanting more than anything to ask what was for dinner, but remembering what Cynthia had said. I had more important things to think about than my empty stomach.

I grabbed Cynthia's arm, almost pulling her out of her old shoes, and ran down the hallway, finding Bess's bedroom at the end on the right. It felt strange being in my grandmother's childhood room and seeing how she lived when she was my age. At least now it was clear where I got my messy habits. I searched through the piles of clothes on the floor and then in the drawers looking for something that didn't look like it had been slept in the night before. I finally settled on a white ruffled blouse and long gray skirt.

As I casually glanced up, I caught a reflection in the ornately carved mirror that was sitting on top of the antique dresser, and what I saw took my breath away. I quickly turned toward Cynthia and, to my relief, I saw my friend of twelve years. But when I looked back into the mirror, I saw a face that wasn't mine–a face I recognized as that of my grandmother when she was a young girl.

I threw out my hand and motioned frantically for Cynthia since I didn't trust myself to speak. She walked toward me with a puzzled look on her face, and then turned completely white as she stared into the mirror. To her shock, staring back was the youthful face of her grandmother, Clara.

Breathing once again, I said hoarsely, "Well, I guess that explains one thing. When we travel back in time through the trunk, we don't just kind of resemble our grandmothers while dressed up in their clothes…to everyone who sees us, we physically *change* into Clara and Bess."

"B…b…but…" Cynthia frantically looked back and forth from me to the mirror, "Gus, you look like *you*, not like…that!"

I couldn't explain it either. "I don't know why our looks remain the same to each other, but the image in the mirror must be how we appear to everyone else. I guess we shouldn't be so surprised.

After all, Biff seemed to recognize me, and Grand-Mama Marie Julia certainly knows what her own daughter looks like!"

"Whatever's happening, the sooner you get Bess's clothes on, the sooner we can get out of here. All we need is for our *twins* to come bouncing into the house," Cynthia said softly.

I quickly got dressed, completing this "stunning" outfit with a pair of hideous mud-covered brown shoes similar to the ones Cynthia was wearing. They were a little too small for my size eight feet, but I'd just have to put up with the pain until I could get back into my comfortable old sneakers.

Before leaving the room, Cynthia and I looked at each other and couldn't help giggling hysterically. We looked like something out of…well…our grandmothers' day! But we didn't have time to stand there and admire ourselves–there was serious work to do, and we weren't sure how much time was left to do it. All I knew was that we had to leave my grandmother's house for now, much to my disappointment.

I grabbed the sailor dress and we slipped out the kitchen door, around the side of the house, and made our way back down the steep hill. Taking one last look, I saw Biff standing on the porch, wagging his tail until we were out of sight. I vowed someday to go back and learn more about my grandmother, Bess; my great-grandmother, Marie Julia; and the rest of the family.

As we walked down the street, I must have been so deep in thought that I didn't notice a girl pedaling toward me on an old fashioned bicycle–at least I didn't notice her until I stepped right into her path. At the very last minute, I looked up to see her swerve to miss me and go tumbling head over heels into a huge mulberry bush.

I rushed over to help her up. "Are you all right? I'm so sorry, but I didn't see you until it was too late to get out of your way."

She was slowly getting up, brushing the dirt off her dress, and picking the branches out of her bright red hair, when she looked up and gasped. My mind raced as I stood there trying to figure out how to explain to my grandmother why she was face to face with herself. Bess's face turned ashen like she was going to faint at any moment, and I must admit I almost hoped she would so I could make a clean getaway.

But all I could do was stand there and stammer, "I…uh…this must be a little…uh…" Fortunately, Cynthia grabbed me before I could make things even worse and hissed, "We've gotta get out of here fast! Look!"

I turned in the direction she was pointing and saw another bicycle rider pedaling furiously up the street in our direction, and she didn't look happy after seeing her friend tumble into the bush.

"Bess! Are you all right? Who are you?" she

yelled at us.

As I watched her getting closer and closer I whispered, "Oh, great! Just what we need to complicate things even more…Clara."

"Let's go," Cynthia snapped.

Somehow I finally got my legs to move and we took off running down the street with our heads hanging as low as possible. We swiftly passed a very angry Clara, making sure that at least *she* wouldn't see our faces, and leaving poor Bess alone to explain what caused her accident.

Chapter Eight

Back in Cynthia's attic, we stashed our grandmothers' old-fashioned clothes in the trunk.

"I don't think we should risk another trip today, do you?" Cynthia sighed, the exhaustion evident in her voice.

"I'm too tired to go anywhere," I groaned. "And we don't want to take the chance of being missed," I added, although time barely moved when we were gone. Besides, it was dinnertime and I was starved, although I couldn't help but picture the delicious meal I was missing at my great-grandmother's house. It was common family knowledge that she'd been a great cook.

Unanimously deciding to stay home for the night, I flew down the street and into my front door. "Oh good," I said eagerly. "Lights are on in the kitchen, and I smell food!" I ran to the table and sat down to…liver and onions. Yuck! No human being, especially a starving kid, should be forced to eat this! Staring at that disgusting plate, I found myself wishing I'd brought Biff back with me. He would've loved it!

After burying as much liver as I could manage under the lettuce in my salad bowl, I excused myself, ran to my room, and fell into an exhausted sleep filled with strange and disturbing dreams–no doubt caused by the liver and onions. I dreamed I was again in Cynthia's attic, and there was a second stairway leading to a closed door. I cautiously walked up this new set of steps and was just getting ready to open the door when I heard a bell ringing in the distance that kept getting louder and louder. Then, over the noise of the bell, I began to hear an eerie voice demanding, *"Look for the bell...look for the bell...look for the bell."* Then, just as I started to run back down these mysterious stairs, frantically trying to escape the ear-piercing sound of the irritating bell, I awoke with a start and found myself on the floor with the alarm clock beside me ringing loudly in my ear.

Coming out of a thick, sleepy haze, I squinted to see what time it was since the sun was barely peeking through the bedroom window. It was not quite seven o'clock, a totally ridiculous hour! Climbing back into bed, I pulled the covers firmly over my head. Then, my memory woke up.

"Oh, no," I groaned, and threw back the covers. Cynthia and I had decided to have an early planning session, which was why I'd set the alarm in the first place. I couldn't decide which was worse…losing a couple of precious hours of sleep, or having Cynthia nag me the rest of the day for being late. Finally dragging my "not a morning person" body out of bed, I hurriedly got dressed feeling as if I hadn't had any rest at all. Apparently I'd been running around an attic all night in my dreams, but now wasn't the time for my fuzzy brain to try to make any sense of it.

"I'm going to Cynthia's," I yelled, running quickly out the front door so my mother wouldn't have time to call me back for breakfast.

I was fast, but not fast enough.

"Augusta Lee," she called. "You need to eat before you go running off!"

"I'm not hungry." I continued down the sidewalk. "Oh, yeah, Gus. Like anyone would believe that!"

I got to Cynthia's house and knocked on the door. Her mother answered and informed me I'd have to get Cynthia out of bed. Oh, great–*I* get up at the crack of dawn and *she's* sleeping in.

"*Cyn...thi...a*," I yelled, bounding up the stairs. "Get up! We have work to do!"

"*Mmm*?" came the sleepy response. "Oh, hi Gus. Sorry I overslept." She yawned, rubbing her eyes. "I was having the weirdest dream about trying to get away from some loud, annoying sound. Oh, and I remember climbing a spooky set of stairs."

"The sound wasn't a very loud bell, was it?" I asked, almost afraid to hear the answer.

"Yeah! How'd you know?" Cynthia sat upright with a puzzled look on her face.

"Because I had the same dream! Now get out of bed and get dressed! I didn't miss breakfast just to

63

sit here and watch you sleep!"

As I sat impatiently watching Cynthia pick out the perfect outfit, slowly brush her hair, and tie a ribbon around a meticulously neat ponytail, I found myself wondering if our dreams meant that we were going to have some new obstacle to tackle in our quest for the missing locket.

"Good grief, Cynthia, *now* what?" I groaned, standing at the bathroom door and shaking my head in exasperation. "Are you actually combing your *eyebrows*?"

"What's wrong with that?" she asked, calmly turning once again toward the bathroom mirror. "I apparently tossed and turned all night and they're just a mess this morning."

I rolled my eyes, but bit my tongue as she squeaked an index finger across her sparkling white teeth and announced that she was ready to face the day.

"Finally," I muttered, "we can concentrate on something important."

After discussing our identical disturbing dreams about the bell and the staircase, we made our way cautiously to the attic. To our relief—or maybe disappointment—everything looked just the way we'd left it the night before. Cynthia and I had no idea what we were going to look for back at Clara's house, but decided that just sitting around all day worrying was not an option.

We got dressed in our magical outfits—I put on

my hat and Cynthia her flowered tiara–and waited for the expected flight through the trunk. Nothing happened.

"What's wrong?" I cried impatiently. "We have on the right clothes and hats."

She was busy digging around in the trunk to see if we'd missed anything when I noticed the attic getting very cold and hazy. The fog became so thick we couldn't see from one end to the other, then we heard a strange noise…a scraping sound coming from the other end of the room. Cynthia grabbed my hand and we stood deathly still.

"*Gus,*" Cynthia whispered. "W…w…what is that?"

I looked in the direction she was pointing just as the fog was starting to clear. To my amazement and terror, a staircase had come right out of the wall...and there was a door at the top just like the one in my dream!

"So…now what do we do?" I asked fearfully, hoping the answer was to run out of the attic as fast as our legs could carry us.

"Cynthia? Do you hear me?" I'm not sure if she did or not because she was standing there with her mouth open and her face white as a sheet.

Although we couldn't feel ourselves moving, we were helplessly drawn to the staircase at the opposite end of the attic. There we stood, knowing we had no other choice but to walk up those stairs and open the door that had beckoned us in our dreams.

"Who's…going first?" I asked anxiously, praying it wasn't going to be me.

"I…I'll go," stammered Cynthia, sounding much braver than her shaky voice revealed. "This is my attic, so I suppose it's only right that I should be the first one to die."

"Oh, *that's* comforting," I said. "Could you get me any more scared than I am already?"

Her eyes flashed with a mixture of annoyance and fear as she began walking slowly but surely up the stairs, with me following at a safe distance. The steps seemed to go on forever! They didn't look that high when we were standing on the attic floor, but we just kept climbing and climbing and climbing until we finally reached the top.

Chapter Nine

Cynthia stood on the final step of the mysterious staircase with her hand on the brass doorknob. "Do you think I should knock?" She chuckled nervously.

After turning the knob and slowly opening the door, we walked straight into...Cynthia's attic!

"This can't be my attic," Cynthia said anxiously. "None of our old stuff is here. The boxes are gone, the tricycles aren't in the corner, and all our old Christmas toys are missing too."

She didn't recognize the attic, but *I* did. "See that cradle over there by the stairway? I almost tripped over it when I was running from Nana Anna." I chuckled, and then slowly started walking toward the center of the room. "There is one thing you'll recognize, besides the cobwebs, of course." I motioned for her to follow me. "Here's a trunk. We don't know if we can use it, but it looks like the same one I used to get back home."

Cynthia sighed with relief that at least something looked familiar, and then said, "This is too weird, Gus. On one side of the door is my attic, and on the other side of the door is this old attic!"

"Clever observation," I muttered under my

breath as I turned around to close the door. That's when I noticed that the attic we just came from was gone! The stairs led down to the second floor of a house. What in the world was happening?

I calmly broke the news. "*Cynthia!* Come *here!* I'm not sure where we are anymore! Your *attic's* gone! We're going to be stuck here forever! We'll *never* get back!"

Well, maybe I wasn't that calm, but fortunately Cynthia kept a cool head as she peeked down the stairs. "It's Clara's house, you lunatic," she hissed. "Now be quiet before someone hears you!"

We listened for any sounds coming from the second floor, then slowly and as quietly as possible, tiptoed down the stairs and into Clara's bedroom. "Yep. This is Clara's house all right. It looks just the way it did when Nana Anna was yelling at you…er, Clara…or whichever one of you lost the locket," I observed.

"Well, *I* certainly didn't lose it," Cynthia stated indignantly. "I wasn't even born yet. My *mother* wasn't even born when that locket was lost!"

"Whatever." I wasn't in the mood to argue about it. The locket had disappeared *sometime* in this century, and life as we knew it might have disappeared forever. I couldn't help wishing we hadn't rushed into using the new staircase because the stairway to Cynthia's attic had vanished and we were quite possibly cut off from our escape home.

As we argued back and forth about where we

were, we didn't notice that someone had quietly walked up the stairs. Before we could react, Nana Anna came straight into Clara's room, put some clean clothes in the top dresser drawer, smoothed the spread, fluffed the pillows, and walked right back out the door without saying a word to us. In fact, she looked straight *through* us! I waited until she'd gone downstairs, then whispered, "Do you think she saw us?"

"How could she miss us?" Cynthia hissed. "She saw us before. Believe me, I'll never forget her yelling right into my face. Why didn't she ignore me *then*?"

All at once we heard the sound of footsteps on the stairs, along with excited, high-pitched laughter. Our reactions were a little better this time as we managed to hide behind Clara's bedroom door just before Clara and Bess came running through.

Oh, no! They're closing the door! They're going to see us! But to my surprise, they jumped on Clara's bed and went on talking as if we weren't even there.

Flattened up against the wall, I knew we had to say something before we scared them to death, especially after our earlier encounter with Bess on the street.

"H…h…hello. W…we don't want to frighten you, but…"

They didn't even look up! Their heads were bent close together as they started whispering, with a giggle thrown in here and there.

I started waving my arms, but they didn't even notice. "Clara and Bess have no idea we're here," I whispered, for no reason since it appeared that they couldn't see *or* hear us. *We must be invisible!*

"Could it have something to do with the fact that we used the magic stairway instead of the trunk to get here?" Cynthia asked. "And the fact that we're wearing different clothes–but I don't know why that would make a difference. Maybe this time we're supposed to slip in and out without being seen."

I had no problem accepting that explanation, especially since, after the first trip, I'd quit trying to make any sense of this whole experience.

We tried to hear what Bess and Clara were saying, which wasn't easy since they were talking so low we had to strain to hear them.

"Oh, you should see it, Bess. It's the most beautiful locket *ever*. I'll bet it's the only locket in the whole world that's shaped like a bell," Clara whispered. "It's gold, with Aunt Belle's initial engraved in the middle of it, and inside are two pictures."

"You just have to show it to me, Clara," Bess insisted.

Clara shook her head, no. "I can't. Mother keeps it hidden away in her dresser drawer and told me never to touch it. But I don't understand why. I think she's being selfish and just doesn't want anyone else in the family to be able to appreciate it."

"So, if she's just being selfish...then we have every right to see how beautiful the locket is," Bess reasoned. "Besides, wouldn't it be nice to see something that belonged to your Aunt Belle since you never got to see *her*?"

Right on cue we heard Nana Anna call from the kitchen, "Clara, will you come downstairs please? I need you to go to the market for me."

Clara jumped up and ran out of the room with Bess in close pursuit. We heard my grandmother insisting all the way down the stairs, "When we get back, you must promise to show me the locket! After all, I'm your best friend, and I deserve to see it before anyone else."

Hmmm...it seemed that my grandmother was quite a manipulator. Maybe I should take notes.

"Gus, I think I just figured out what's going on," Cynthia said thoughtfully. "The last time we were in this house, Mama Clara had already lost the locket. But for some reason, this time we've come back *before* it disappeared, which means we might be here to keep her from losing it."

I didn't know if we could or not, but one thing was certain–we were going to have to keep a close eye on Bess and Clara if there was any chance of keeping the locket safe.

Chapter Ten

After Clara and Bess left on their errand, we went into Nana Anna's room and rooted through the dresser until we found the box containing the locket tucked away in the bottom drawer. Relieved that Clara hadn't somehow sneaked it out from under our noses before leaving the house, we carefully opened the box and unwrapped the white tissue paper that contained the treasure.

"It's beautiful," I murmured. "No wonder Clara and Bess couldn't resist it."

Cynthia stood there quietly, gently cradling the locket in her hand, rubbing her finger over the delicately engraved *B*. She opened it up, looking first at the picture of Nana Anna, then at the face that looked eerily like her own, saying softly, "I feel like I finally met Aunt Belle."

"Should we just hide it from Clara and Bess until they lose interest?" I asked.

"That won't work," Cynthia said firmly, "because your grandmother is dying to get her hands on it, and besides, we can't stay here guarding it forever."

"We'll just have to follow Clara around to make sure she doesn't lose it again," I said, not quite sure how we could keep that from happening.

Reluctantly putting the locket back in the drawer for safekeeping, we decided to snoop around in the attic for any clues that might help us get back home once we're sure the locket is safe.

The first thing we did was open the old trunk just to be sure the locket hadn't mysteriously found its way into the attic while we weren't looking. After all, stranger things had happened! It wasn't there, but as we found ourselves going through the trunk, Cynthia asked, "Didn't Mama Clara say that these old furs and most of the clothes were thrown out not long after the locket disappeared?"

"I think so," I answered, trying to remember exactly what Cynthia's grandmother had told us about the contents of the trunk. "Yes. She told us that it was almost empty except for the ballet dress Nana Anna stored in it after the locket disappeared. Why?"

Cynthia crossed her arms and stared thoughtfully into the trunk. "I just can't understand what could've happened to the locket when Clara went back to look for it."

I'd been silently making a long list of all the things *I* didn't understand.

As we continued looking through the clothes in the trunk, a piece of paper fell out of the pocket of one of the furs. "Hey, Cynthia. Look at this. It's an old ticket of some kind…a steamship ticket from England to America."

"*Hmmm…*" she said, taking the ticket. "I'm pretty sure this isn't the year Nana Anna and her family came here…the ticket is dated several years later." All of a sudden, I saw her face light up. "Gus, do you think this might be the one that Nana Anna sent to Belle before the locket disappeared?"

Before I could answer, we heard noises downstairs and realized that the girls must be back from their errand. "Time to go to work," I sighed. "We can't let that locket *or* Clara and Bess out of our sight."

Cynthia threw the ticket back into the trunk and we made our way downstairs, getting to Clara's bedroom at about the same time they did. There was nothing to do but stand guard at the door and try to find out what their plans were for sneaking the locket out of Nana Anna's dresser. Fortunately, we didn't have to wait long.

"Clara, I'm going next door to see Mrs. Winters for a few minutes. Stay here while I'm gone," Nana Anna called from the kitchen. Without waiting for an answer, we heard the screen door slam as she left.

Bess looked at Clara with a devilish gleam in her eye. "Here's our chance. It'll take old Mrs. Winters half an hour just to show your mom the new quilt she's working on. Let's go get the locket before she comes back."

We watched as, having lost all resistance, Clara raced into her mother's bedroom, opened the drawer, and snatched the box. Bess tried to grab it out of her hands, but Clara said firmly, "No, not here! Let's go up to the attic so we won't get caught."

They ran up the stairs to the attic, with Cynthia and me in close pursuit.

The two of them sat down on the dusty floor, and Clara carefully untied the satin ribbon and opened the box that held the precious locket. "It's even more spectacular than you described, Clara. Please let me try it on," Bess begged, grabbing for the locket.

"After me," Clara demanded. "It's my locket, so I'll go first. At least it *will* be mine when I can convince my mother I'm old enough to wear it."

As Clara was admiring the locket, Bess walked toward the trunk. "Who's been up here? The trunk's open, and it looks like someone was going through the clothes."

Cynthia and I glanced at each other, then at the trunk. Oops. We'd forgotten to put the clothes back.

"Oh, Mother's been threatening to throw away half the stuff up here, so maybe she's been sorting through things. She says at least twice a year that she's going to clean the attic, but it never gets done." Clara chuckled, as she slipped the locket and chain over her head.

She struck a pose and asked, "So, how do I look?"

"Here, put this fur on and then I'll tell you,"

ordered Bess.

Clara stood up, wrapped the fur around her shoulders, and started strutting around the attic like a fashion model. They were having such a good time trying on all the old clothes and admiring the locket that they didn't hear Clara's mother coming up the attic stairs. Neither did we—and we should've known, from Mama Clara's story, to expect her.

"What are you two doing up here?" Nana Anna demanded.

I thought we were going to have to peel Clara off the ceiling!

"What! Oh…uh…hello, Mother. I was just showing Bess all the old clothes that you're thinking of getting rid of," Clara replied, her voice sounding about three octaves higher than normal as she tightly clutched the fur around her neck.

"Well, go downstairs right now," she said impatiently. "This attic is too messy and dirty for the two of you to be playing here. And put all those clothes back in the trunk." She stood there, arms folded, waiting for Clara and Bess to clean up their mess.

As Bess was quickly gathering the rest of the clothes that were scattered on the floor, Clara turned her back to Nana Anna, slipped the fur over her head, along with the locket, and threw them both into the trunk before her mother had a chance to see what she had around her neck. Bess quickly snatched the box off the floor, threw it in the trunk, closed the lid, and the two girls meekly followed Clara's mother downstairs.

"Well," I said, running toward the trunk, "this should be a piece of cake! The locket won't get lost this time." I opened the trunk lid, and Cynthia and I started hunting for it. The box was right on top where Bess threw it, but the locket was nowhere to be found.

"It must've slipped in between the clothes," Cynthia said with little confidence, as we continued to search.

We took everything out of the trunk–except the locket!

"Where is it? How could it get lost?" I cried, totally frustrated. "Oh, this can't be happening again."

Not only had the locket disappeared for a second time, but the attic fog rolled in just as before, and our magic stairway reappeared.

"Well, it looks like there's someplace we're supposed to go," Cynthia's voice trembled.

Even though we were being drawn to the staircase once again, we were torn between wanting to see where it would lead this time and continuing our exasperating hunt for the locket.

"Well, I'm positive that locket isn't in the trunk," Cynthia said. "So maybe the appearance of the stairway is a sign that we need to look for more clues. Besides, I don't know how you feel, but this seems like a demand rather than a request."

I couldn't dispute that. When a stairway magically appears before your eyes, you'd be pretty stupid not to realize there's a darn good reason. Besides, this might be the perfect time to test whether going up the stairway instead of through the trunk really made us invisible instead of simply turning us into Clara and Bess impersonators.

Chapter Eleven

Once more, we made our way up the long staircase to the door at the top. Cynthia was just getting ready to turn the handle when I interrupted.

"Uh…Cynthia, maybe…you should knock this time." What I saw made the little hairs on my neck stand straight out. The brass doorknocker just above Cynthia's head was shaped like a *bell,* with the initial *B* engraved in the middle.

Cynthia's hand shook as she reached up. "It's a b…bell," she gulped. "Do you think it's connected to the one we heard in our dreams?"

Before I could answer, the door slowly swung open on its own. We took one last look at each other and walked cautiously into a small but cheerful-looking cottage with large bay windows that overlooked a beautiful green meadow. The furniture was old and faded, but warm and inviting, and on the floor was a flowered rug that appeared to be woven with every color of the rainbow.

A Steinway grand piano stood in one corner of the room, with a vase of bright pink roses sitting on a small brass table to the left. Hanging on the pale green walls, just above the table, a painting of a ballerina in soft pink pastel tones caught my eye.

As I looked more closely, I noticed the dancer had on the same ballet dress that Cynthia and I had found in the trunk…and a bell-shaped locket was around her neck.

Staring so intently at the picture, I wasn't aware that a woman had appeared from nowhere. My head spun around at the same time Cynthia gave me a very painful poke in the ribs.

"*Ow*," I cried involuntarily the moment I saw this stranger standing in the middle of the room. She chuckled softly and smiled at the two of us. I had the feeling I'd seen her before, but couldn't place where. Her light brown hair was pulled softly back from her heart-shaped face, and was loosely tied with a pink satin ribbon. She practically floated over to us as she held out her hand. It was then I realized why she looked familiar to me…she was the woman in the painting, and she looked just like Cynthia.

"You're Isabelle," I blurted out loud. I figured that I'd have to do all the talking since Cynthia appeared to be in a state of shock.

"Yes," she answered, with an almost angelic voice. "I've been expecting you."

"You've been expecting us? Does that mean you know who we are?" I asked, somewhat surprised.

"Of course," she said softly. "You, my dear, are Augusta Lee, and your silent sidekick is my great-great-niece, Cynthia," she chuckled, and added cheerfully, "I'm also quite aware of why you're here.

Now, sit down before you faint."

I started to correct Aunt Belle and demand that she call me "Gus," but for the first time in my life, I actually liked being called Augusta Lee. This elegant lady made it sound enchanting. I grabbed Cynthia's arm and led her over to a plush, emerald green loveseat. I couldn't help but think that this must be what it feels like to sit on a cloud. Even the chairs in Cynthia's den weren't this soft and comforting.

"I've been waiting for someone to take this journey, and you two didn't disappoint me," Belle said.

"So, are you the one who's behind all these wild trips back and forth to Mama Clara's house, and…wherever we are now?" Cynthia looked around, finally acknowledging her surroundings.

"In a way, Cynthia," Belle said, "but I had help. You two girls created this adventure from your desire to ease Clara's guilt about losing the locket, along with your imaginations that made you believe that nothing was impossible. Each problem you encountered along the way allowed you to create a solution that led you to me, and to the answer you need in order to solve the mystery of the lost locket."

"So…are you saying that this is our final destination?" I asked anxiously.

"Well, if you're asking if you have to stay here the rest of your lives," she said patiently, "then I don't believe this is your *final* destination. You need to find the locket first, and then I'm sure you two will be able to find your way back home."

I was getting a little edgy with all this talk about going home, and was anxious to find out from Aunt Belle why we were there, and what we were supposed to do next. "So, Aunt Belle, uh…er…may I call you Aunt Belle?"

"Of course, Augusta Lee." She smiled. "Or would you rather I called you 'Gus?'"

"Oh, no," I answered quickly. "Augusta Lee is just fine."

Cynthia stared at me in disbelief as Belle continued. "I would imagine you're a little anxious to know exactly why you're here."

She must be psychic, or maybe it's just that I've never been very good at hiding my feelings. Whatever, it must've worked because she finally began weaving a story that even Cynthia and I couldn't have dreamed up.

"I might as well start with the locket since that's your purpose for being here. I had it made," she began, "soon after my family left on their voyage to America. I was miserable those first few months without my mother and father, and especially without my dear sister, Anna. That's why I wanted the locket, so I could at least keep her picture close to my heart. I also spent much of the time practicing after joining the ballet company. Finally, after several years of struggle, I'd been promised the lead in one of the ballets for the upcoming season. My destiny was clear, or so I thought, until I met Andre. He was the most handsome man I'd ever seen, and I became totally captivated by his charm and devotion to me."

When Cynthia and I heard this, we looked at each other, amazed that someone as smart and talented as Belle would let anyone interfere with her dancing. At our age, we were just starting to accept the fact that boys actually had a reason for being, but would've never considered letting one come between us and a lifelong dream. What in the world was she thinking?

She went on to say that the next six months were the happiest of her life. Andre was an artist and spent his days painting portraits and landscapes, and then selling them on the streets of Paris. Belle was always by his side.

"It was during this time," she explained, "that he painted the portrait that's hanging on the wall. He said that from the first moment he saw me, he'd become obsessed with painting a ballerina. I gave my consent, but insisted I wear the locket in the portrait because it was as much a part of me as the color of my eyes. That's when I got the idea to send the gifts to Anna. I would always have the portrait, and she would have my favorite ballet dress and most prized possession…the locket."

Belle walked over to a red velvet chair and sat down. All of a sudden, she had become very quiet, as if she were having a difficult time continuing the story. Cynthia got up from the loveseat and walked over to her, sitting down on the soft rug beside the chair.

"You don't have to go on if you don't want to," Cynthia said quietly, taking Belle's hand.

They made quite a pair–almost like mother and daughter, although Belle appeared much too young to be Cynthia's mother. Maybe *sisters* would be a better description. Whatever their relationship, it was obvious they had formed an immediate bond.

Belle smiled down at Cynthia and said, "Thank you for being so sensitive, dear, but I need to finish the story so we can all be on our way."

I wanted to ask what she meant by that, but Belle continued. "Soon after Andre finished my portrait, he began distancing himself from me, staying away for days, and when I did see him, he was very vague about where he'd been. The harder I tried to become close to him, the more he pulled away. I was deep in thought, walking down the street one day, when a new painting in a shop window caught my eye. It was a portrait of a very beautiful, young lady, painted recently, and signed by Andre. I was devastated."

"When he came over that evening, we had a terrible argument when I asked him about her, but afterward he begged me to give him one more chance. However, I had begun to realize that he wasn't any more in love with me than he was with that other young woman–he had just been in love with the idea of painting me." After a long pause, Belle continued, "I wanted to give him another chance, but I told him that I just didn't think I could trust him anymore. He was very angry when he left and vowed that one day I'd be sorry."

Cynthia and I had tears in our eyes. I couldn't imagine what Belle must have gone through, but it was clear that the experience with Andre was still very painful to her.

"Mama Clara told us that no one in the family ever heard from you again. What happened? Where did you go?" I felt a little guilty about asking questions that might add to her anguish.

"Since I was hurt and ashamed over being such a fool, I couldn't face telling my family. I left Paris and traveled the countryside until I found this little cottage. The moment I walked through the door, I felt I was walking into heaven, and spent the next several years making a completely new life for myself. However, the guilt of hurting my family by disappearing never went away. I tried several times to write just to let them know I was alive and well, but as time passed, my new life took over and my old life seemed farther and farther away. So I just put my past, including my family, behind me." She looked down at the floor and continued, "If I could, that would be the one thing in my life I'd change."

She paused for a moment, then went on, "But enough about me. You're here to help Clara, so you need to find the locket, right?"

We nodded. "We thought we knew exactly where it was, but when we went back for it, the locket had disappeared just as it did the first time Clara threw it into the trunk," I said, hoping that Belle might be able to help us solve the mystery.

"It was in the trunk all the time, but Clara missed it and so did the two of you," Belle said.

"It can't be," Cynthia argued. "We took everything out of that trunk and it's not there!"

"Yes, it is," Belle said patiently. "It's in the lining of the fur that Clara tried on with the locket that day." She went on to explain that when Nana Anna caught Clara and Bess with the locket, Clara panicked. She hurriedly threw the fur and the locket into the trunk, not realizing that the locket had slipped into a tear in the lining of the fur.

"The fur," Cynthia and I both exclaimed.

"Yes, but it won't be there long," Belle insisted. "You need to find it at once or it *will* disappear–this time for good. The fur was given away not long after the locket was lost, and it will be again if you don't hurry."

"How did you know where the locket was, Aunt Belle?" I asked.

"There just isn't enough time to go into that, Augusta Lee. All you need to know is that, although I put my family through much anguish when I disappeared, now I'm always watching over them. You really must hurry. Time may be standing still for you, but it isn't for Clara."

"But what about you?" Cynthia asked. "Why don't you come with us?"

Belle shook her head. "I don't have a way to go back with you...not yet. Don't worry about me. I have a feeling I'll be able to return when the time is right."

"Well then, in the meantime, can we come back to see you?" I asked. "I know there are so many stories we'd love to hear...if you're willing to tell us, that is."

"You can come back after you've recovered the locket," Belle reassured us, "and then we can talk for as long as you wish until the time comes for you to go home. Just go back the way you came and you'll find yourselves in Clara's attic."

Chapter Twelve

Cynthia and I ran out of the cottage door, down the stairs, and into Clara's attic, just as Belle had promised. We threw open the trunk, took out the fur, and started searching through the torn lining.

"It's here," Cynthia said excitedly. "Just where Aunt Belle said it would be."

"Should we put it back in Nana Anna's dresser drawer, or leave it here and hope that Clara has enough sense to find it this time?" I asked. "I think it would be better if Clara has a chance to find it."

"Let's just put the locket back in the trunk so it can't possibly be missed," Cynthia said. "Then I think we should stay here, stand guard, and hope that Clara comes looking for it."

We both agreed we hadn't come that far to let the locket out of our sight for one second.

We put it back in the trunk so it could be easily found, then entertained ourselves for a while by talking about everything we were going to do when we got home. "I can't wait to run to across the street to the gas station and get an Orange Crush out of the vending machine," I said longingly, thinking how great it would taste right that moment. Cynthia couldn't wait to take a hot bubble bath. "Danielle got this new bath oil for getting straight A's on her report card, and has been making me sick all week with her bragging," she sniffed angrily. "I'd be perfectly justified in using it first."

It was just starting to get dark when we heard the door slowly open and footsteps creep up the stairs. We peeked around an old dusty wool rug that hung, suspended from the ceiling with clothespins, as I pinched my nose tightly shut to keep from sneezing. Even though no one had been able to see us before we visited Aunt Belle, no sense in taking chances.

What a relief...it was Clara. We saw her carefully open the trunk, find the locket, and breathe a very heavy sigh of relief as she turned to make her way back down the stairway. We decided to follow just to be sure she returned it to her mother's dresser drawer.

As we watched Clara open the drawer and slip the box under a stack of white linen handkerchiefs, Cynthia and I shook hands on a job well done. But there was no time for celebrating, because we were eager to get back to Aunt Belle's.

We ran back up the attic stairs, taking them two at a time in our enthusiasm to see Belle again and hear more stories of her years in Paris. Racing across the floor, we came to a screeching halt as we realized the magic stairway was gone.

"But Aunt Belle promised," Cynthia cried. "She said we could go back as soon as Clara found the locket in the trunk…and now we don't have a way to get there."

We sat down on the dusty floor feeling betrayed. She must've known that the only way we'd agree to leave in time to find the locket was if we truly believed we could return.

"Well, we can't sit here and mope for the rest of our lives," I sighed, slowly getting to my feet. "We only have one option." I walked over to the trunk and pessimistically opened the lid. "Oh, just great. I'm standing here in the same outfit that brought me here, but nothing is happening. I'm not being pulled into the trunk, and I'm not on my way back home." I started to cry just thinking about being stuck in a place where no one could see or hear us. What made it worse was Cynthia bent over rummaging through the contents, paying no attention to me.

"Aren't you the least bit concerned?" I sobbed.

"What? Oh…uh…yeah, I'm concerned," she mumbled vaguely, continuing her search through the trunk. After digging for a few more minutes, she triumphantly stood up. "Yes! Here it is…the steamship ticket! This could be the one that was sent to Aunt Belle."

"Yeah, so?" I said indifferently, unable to imagine why a fifty-year-old steamship ticket would be of any use, although…it isn't fifty years old where we are now! "Do you think it's still good?" I asked with sudden interest, hoping it might also be *our* ticket out of here.

"Well," Cynthia said, "there's only one way to find out. We have to somehow get back to Aunt Belle."

As soon as the words were out, we heard a familiar scraping sound and watched the fog start rolling in, which could mean only one thing—our stairway was coming back. We wasted no time running up the steps and through the door that led to Belle's cottage.

She was at the piano when we walked in—completely lost in the classical sounds of Beethoven, or so we thought. Without missing a note or a beat, she said, "*Ahh…*I was hoping you'd find a reason to visit me again."

Walking over to the piano, ticket in hand, Cynthia asked, "Were you serious about wishing you could change the past?"

Belle looked puzzled. "What do you mean?"

"I think we've found a way you can get back in touch with your family. A couple of months before Clara lost the locket, your sister Anna mailed a steamship ticket to you hoping you would agree to visit, and maybe even decide to stay. The ticket, along with a letter, was returned to her because you must've already moved. If this is the same ticket, it may be the connection to your family," Cynthia said hopefully, as she handed the ticket to Belle.

What happened next amazed even two seasoned "trunk travelers." As Belle took the ticket from Cynthia's hand, she disappeared in a shimmering mist right before our eyes.

Cynthia and I stood there for a few minutes, unable to move or speak, until I finally gulped, "Well, I think that was the right ticket." After a moment I added, "So, where do you think she went, and more important, where do *we* go from here? Back to Clara's attic?"

Cynthia nodded. "Until we think of a way to get home, I guess that's as good a place as any. I don't think it's a good idea to stay here, since there's nothing else we can do."

Having made our way out of Belle's cottage and down the stairs into Clara's attic, we felt as if something had gone terribly wrong. For one thing, the attic appeared as if no one had been there in months even though we'd just left. The trunk was, once again, dust-covered without any sign that four curious girls had recently disturbed its contents. Cynthia and I sat there for several minutes fearing that the magic was also gone from the trunk…and afraid to find out because, if that were the case, our transportation home had permanently vanished too.

All of a sudden, sounds from below caught my attention. "Cynthia, listen," I said. "Something's going on downstairs."

We heard troubled voices coming from the foyer as we hurriedly made our way to the top of the stairway leading to the first floor. Looking over the banister down into the foyer, we saw Nana Anna crying, with Clara doing her best to comfort her mother. A telegram was in Clara's hand, and we noticed several pieces of luggage sitting by the front door.

"I don't understand, Mother. What could've happened to Aunt Belle?" Clara cried as she read the telegram. "She sent this from the ship to let us know that she'd boarded, so why didn't she arrive in New York?"

Nana Anna could only shake her head and say with a trembling voice, "I don't know, Clara. I just don't know. The steamship company said she simply disappeared."

Watching the two of them walk slowly down the hallway and into the kitchen, we decided to go back up to the attic to try to figure out this new crisis, and if we'd somehow been responsible for Belle's disappearance.

We sat on the trunk for several minutes before Cynthia finally cried miserably, "I just don't know what could've gone wrong. I was so sure that Aunt Belle would be able to use the ticket to bring her to America and back to her family…and she was so eager to see her sister again. What stopped her?"

"Maybe we should try to go back to Aunt Belle's cottage and see if she's there. I suppose the stairway could take us…except that it's not here anymore." I looked toward the end of the attic where the stairway had appeared to us, half hoping that just wishing for it would make it materialize…but no such luck. Then I remembered that we'd only been able to go back to see Belle the second time because we had the ticket for her, so there must be something we were supposed to find in order to be able to return. But what could it be?

"Do you think we could find any clues in her luggage that might lead us to where she is, or help us find out what happened to her?" I asked.

Cynthia shrugged and said mournfully, "I don't know. Maybe we should just leave well enough alone. We've made Aunt Belle disappear and now Nana Anna and Clara are more miserable than ever!"

All I could do was sigh as we trudged downstairs, shoulders slumped, wondering what had gone wrong with Aunt Belle's voyage. Or whether she'd even been on the ship.

Searching through the luggage that was still sitting by the front door, we opened the first bag and found nothing but clothing. But in the second one, we noticed a menu and a ship brochure that Belle must've picked up when she boarded. It had all kinds of information about entertainment for the passengers: shuffleboard and bridge tournaments, dancing lessons…along with something else that caught our attention. There was mention at the bottom of the brochure about a French painter who had been commissioned to do portraits for interested ship passengers. The advertisement read *Portraits by Andre*. I looked at Cynthia, almost afraid to ask, "This couldn't possibly be the same Andre…could it?" It just seemed too incredible to even consider. But that was the only clue we could find in the luggage, so we took it. I decided to grab the ship's menu as we made our way back to the attic so I could torture myself by reading descriptions of all the mouth-watering food and sinful desserts.

As we were walking up the stairs, Cynthia said, "If this is a clue about Aunt Belle's disappearance, we'll probably know right away." That's when we heard scraping noises coming from the attic above us. It sounded like our question had been answered. Our stairway was back.

Chapter Thirteen

We weren't the least bit surprised when we found the magic stairway right there waiting for us, but where we ended up was a *huge* surprise. Going through the door, we expected to find ourselves back in Belle's cottage, but instead landed on the gangplank leading to a large ship.

"Pardon me. Excuse me. Coming through." A man in a black suit carrying a large satchel pushed his way past several dozen passengers trying to board the ship.

"Well, I never! How rude," snorted a rather portly older woman as she tried her best to drag two young children up the steep ramp. "We're *all* trying to board, young man," she shouted.

He stepped onto the ship and disappeared without looking back.

"He seemed to be in a hurry, didn't he?" Cynthia observed.

I was too busy realizing my worst fear! If this ship left the port with us on it, how long could it be before I was *heaving* over the side? I had turned around to run back through the attic door when the gangplank shook violently, which left us no choice but to scurry on board. Just as we made it onto the ship, a deafening, bellowing noise came from the smokestacks. That was the signal that we were–for better or worse–passengers on a very large ship heading out toward the open waters of the Atlantic Ocean.

"So, aren't we supposed to have some kind of boarding pass or ticket to get on this thing?" I murmured, half hoping that if I didn't have one, someone would transport me off this huge, stomach-churning vessel.

"If our theory holds true about the stairway, then just like our second trip to Clara's house, we can't be seen…so no need for a ticket," Cynthia said flippantly.

At that precise moment, a lady in a very large emerald green hat decorated with an even larger plume of ostrich feathers walked right through us!

"Well, I guess that question's been answered." Cynthia shivered. "We not only can't be seen, it's like we're not even here."

"Hey," I said deviously, forgetting my concerns about getting sick, "you know, we could end up having a lot of fun with this."

But before I could dream up any mischief, Cynthia said, "C'mon, Gus. We need to explore the ship and see if we can spot Belle."

The place was crawling with people–standing in line at something called the purser's office or talking excitedly as they climbed the grand staircase; trying to get a good chair out on the deck; checking out the gift shops. In a crowd like this, it's a good thing we didn't have to go around dodging people and could just walk through anyone and anything we wanted. But at the same time, with the huge number of passengers on board, the idea of just bumping into Aunt Belle was getting less and less likely. It appeared that we were going to have to do some investigating to find the location of her cabin.

Cynthia looked one way, then the other. "So where should we go first?"

As I was getting ready to say that I didn't have a clue, the smell of food came drifting down from the hallway straight ahead. *Hey, I'm really hungry. Is it possible I'm not going to get seasick after all?*

"Why don't we start in the dining room?" I suggested eagerly. "After all, everyone has to eat."

"Well, I'd worry about how we were going to find it, Gus," Cynthia said smugly, "but I have a feeling that nose of yours will take us right to the food."

I knew that was supposed to be insulting, but I was so hungry that I didn't even care. Besides, she was right. Back in our neighborhood, I was known for being able to sniff out fresh-baked peanut butter cookies in any kitchen on the block. So it wasn't much of a test for me to get to the dining room without any wrong turns.

As soon as I stepped through the doors I knew it was like nothing I'd ever seen before. The formal dining room had deep red carpeting that was so plush we seemed to sink down to our ankles. The twinkling chandeliers that hung from the ceiling appeared to be larger than my whole bedroom. Most of the tables were still empty since it was just a little early for the noon meal crowd, but food was already being set out onto large buffet tables...and did it ever look good!

I walked over to one of the tables and casually tried to pick up an apple, thinking I could eat it as we walked around the ship looking for Belle. But to my total surprise, my hand went right through it! I tried again...same result.

"Cynthia. Come over here," I pleaded. "I can't pick up this apple."

"Oh, good grief. You're totally helpless," she snapped, walking toward the table.

"Okay, then you try," I challenged. She did, and just like mine, her hand went right through the apple. "We could pick things up at Clara's, so why can't we pick anything up here?"

I was too busy whining to even think. "There's gotta be a way. I'm starving, with all this food right in front of me, and I can't even pick up an apple."

"Maybe if you just concentrate on it." Cynthia sighed impatiently.

"Oh sure, like that's going to help," I mumbled under my breath, knowing it couldn't be as simple as my lack of concentration. Then again, maybe if I just focused on the apple. I tried once more to pick it up...blocking everything else out of my mind.

*Just pick up the apple...just...pick...up...the...apple.
Pick...up...the apple.*

To my total surprise, the apple popped into my hand. "I did it," I yelled with smug satisfaction. But as I playfully tossed it in the air I heard an ear-piercing shriek and the clatter of breaking dishes off to one side. Catching the apple with my left hand, I turned in the direction of the commotion and saw a young woman in a white uniform standing at the door to the kitchen–surrounded by a pile of broken glasses and dishes, screaming her fool head off, and looking straight at my hand. How could she see me? And so what if she did? Surely taking one little apple wasn't reason enough for her to be carrying on this way.

"Uh oh," I said, looking down at the apple. The horrified look on her face made me realize that, from her point of view, an apple had just floated off the tray, shot straight up, back down, and was now suspended in mid-air.

I turned to Cynthia and said frantically, "What should I do? I'm invisible! She can't see anything except this apple flying around!" But she was no help at all, she was doubled over laughing so hard. I wanted to laugh too, and maybe pitch the apple to this poor unsuspecting girl, but then we noticed a crowd gathering and the last thing we needed was to draw attention to ourselves. So I put the apple back down on the tray as inconspicuously as possible, which wasn't easy under the circumstances, and slowly backed away from the table. By the time we reached the dining room door, several people had gathered cautiously around the tray waiting for more "apple tricks."

"I guess we have to be more careful what we pick up from now on," I said. "Did you see the look on her face? I think she would've passed out if I'd thrown it at her."

"It's lucky we got out of there as easily as we did," Cynthia reminded me, spoiling my cheerful mood. "We have to be more careful or people are going to think this cruise ship is haunted and start watching for us. Then we'll never find Aunt Belle."

"Oh, I suppose so," I muttered, having a hard time concentrating on anything serious. I just couldn't help imagining us as ghosts, and all the really cool tricks we could play. However, she was right. Our first priority had to be finding Belle.

"Ya know, we could make this real easy if we could just find the ship's passenger list. I'm sure they have all the names and cabins listed somewhere," I offered, hoping I could convince Cynthia that I'd put all ghostly thoughts out of my mind and was, once again, completely focused on our goal.

Cynthia seemed to be deep in thought and didn't answer, but finally asked, "Gus, do you remember the conversation we overheard at the door when Clara and Nana Anna were talking about Belle's disappearance?"

"Uh, maybe," I said. "What are you thinking about?"

"I'm sure Clara mentioned they'd gotten an earlier telegram from Belle just after she'd boarded the ship. And if she did, then that means we might be able to track her down at the telegraph office…if we only knew where it was."

"Well let's just *ask* somebody," I said impatiently.

"Oh, sure. Let's just go back up to the main lobby and find that guy we saw working in the purser's office and ask him how we can find Aunt Belle's cabin. I'm sure in our present invisible condition we'll get his undivided attention," she said sarcastically.

"Oh, yeah," I said, feeling pretty foolish, but not letting on to her. "Just because I'm not used to being invisible to the entire world doesn't give you the right to yell at me! I just forgot," I snapped.

"Oh, you're just 'dis…*Gus*…ting,'" she said indignantly, as she turned and stomped off in the direction of the Grand Staircase.

"Ha, ha," I sneered. "Like I haven't heard *that* one before."

Cynthia yelled over her shoulder, "Do you want to stay there and talk to yourself, or help me find the telegraph office?"

I didn't even bother to answer. I just walked sullenly behind her thinking how I was going to find myself some new friends when I get home…*if* I get home.

"Hey." There was a tap on my shoulder. Spinning around, I saw a young boy with large, brown, inquisitive eyes standing in the hallway. He was dressed in black pants and white shirt, along with a slightly lopsided brown plaid cap. "Whatcha doin'?" he asked, shuffling his feet nervously, and at the same time pulling on frayed suspenders.

"Huh?" I said impatiently. The last thing I wanted was to be distracted by some bratty little kid.

"Sorry to bother you, but I'm pretty lonely, and I thought maybe I could hang around with you and your friend for a while," he said hopefully.

I was ready to shoo him away when the thought struck. *How can he see me? Has our invisibility worn off?* "Do you see me, kid?" I asked firmly.

"Y–yes," he replied slowly, "the same way you see me. You're dead too…aren't you?"

My humongous gasp almost sent him running. "Wait," I said quickly, "I didn't mean to startle you. It's just not every day I talk to someone who says he's dead." *Nope…not every day.*

"Let's start over," I coaxed. *Try to be patient for once in your life, Gus.* "Now, I believe you mentioned that you're dead. Is that right?"

"Yes," he said, with a little more conviction this time. I stood waiting for him to continue, but it looked like I was going to have to pull the words out. *Remember, Gus…patience.*

"What's going on? And who's this?" Cynthia asked.

"Oh! Geez, Cynthia! Do you have to sneak up on me like that?" I cried.

"I wasn't sneaking up on you. I got tired of waiting by the staircase while you're wasting time talking to some..." Her voice trailed off as she realized that no one–even this boy–should be able to see us.

"Uh...Gus. Can I talk to you a minute...over here?" Cynthia motioned, the pitch of her voice noticeably higher.

"What's going on?" she hissed when we were out of earshot. "Who is he?"

Deciding to have a little fun I calmly answered, "Oh, he's a ghost."

"A *what*?" she yelled.

"*Shh*. He's a very skittish ghost. You'll scare him." I choked down a laugh. Cynthia just stood there, shoulders slumped and her mouth hanging open. I'd probably pushed her as far as I dared. She was starting to look a little scary herself.

"You really know as much as I do," I confessed. "He just came up to me and started talking like any normal person–well, except for the fact that he's dead."

"Why didn't you just say so, Gus," Cynthia said sarcastically. "I thought something *weird* was going on."

"Excuse me," the boy broke in, "I'll just be

going now. I don't want to cause any trouble." He turned and started walking dejectedly down the hallway.

I pleaded silently to Cynthia, and she nodded in agreement. "Hey kid," I said cheerfully, "c'mon back. We'd like you to hang around with us."

Chapter Fourteen

We found out that his name was Louis and that his father was the ship's captain. "I used to beg to go with him," he explained, "but my mother always said 'no.' I missed my dad so much because he was gone most of the time."

"That's sad, Louie," I said sympathetically, thinking how lucky I was that my dad was home every night.

"It's *Louis*," he said firmly.

"Ha, Gus! Looks like you're getting a little of your own medicine," Cynthia laughed.

I made a face at her, and then turned my attention back to Louis. "Sorry, Louis. I didn't mean to offend you. By the way, I'm Gus, and this is Cynthia. And we're not dead."

"We're here to find my Aunt Belle," Cynthia chimed in. "Maybe you can help us. Have you by any chance seen a young woman, oh…about this tall," she held her arm as far over her head as she could reach, "with light brown hair and blue eyes?"

Louis rolled his eyes. "I've probably seen a hundred women who look like that."

Cynthia crossed her arms defensively and sniffed, "I didn't think it would hurt to ask."

"How long have you been on the ship?" I asked.

He sighed and then answered, "I'm not quite sure, but it's been at least five years. I know because they have a birthday party on the ship for my dad every year, and I've counted up to five."

"So, you've gone to all the parties?" Cynthia asked. "Does your dad know you're there?"

"Yeah, I've been to every one of them, and sometimes he acts like he knows I'm there, but…oh, I'm just not sure," answered Louis sadly. "I used to try to talk to him, but I didn't get any response, so I finally gave up."

Cynthia asked the question I'd been wanting to, but didn't have the nerve. "How did you, uh…die, Louis?"

"Dad finally convinced Mom to let me go with him on just one voyage," he began. "I was so happy. I had the run of the ship, and even got to take the wheel," he said excitedly.

Hmmm, I thought. *He must know this boat inside out.*

Louis continued, "We were just three days out of port when I got sick. The doctor said it was 'the Fever.'"

"Scarlet, Typhoid, or Smallpox?" I questioned.

"I think it was Typhoid Fever," he answered. "I can remember the doctor saying that it was 'bad luck' because hardly anyone got sick with it anymore, but I caught it sometime before we left America, and there was nothing anyone could do for me." His voice trailed off, and he slumped against the wall.

It impressed me that someone so young could be so matter-of-fact about his own death. Although I wanted to find out more, I had a feeling that Louis was wearing down. Besides, I thought we might be able to use his expertise in finding Belle.

"Say, Louis. Would you happen to know if there's a telegraph office on board?" I asked, hopefully.

A look of revelation on Cynthia's face indicated that it had also dawned on her that Louis might be just what we needed to find some answers.

"Yeah, sure," he answered. "The telegraph officer is a nervous little guy, and he hardly ever goes out on deck. I think he even sleeps there."

Guess that rules out sneaking in there at night. We'll just have to be careful when we're there so we don't rouse suspicion.

"It's been great small-talking, Louis," Cynthia said abruptly, "but we need to find the telegraph office and my great-aunt, and we're not going to accomplish either one by standing here in the hall."

"I'll help...if you want," Louis said shyly. "At least I can show you where it is."

With Louis leading the way, we walked up the Grand Staircase, onto a deck, up more stairs, and then out on to something with a gross-sounding name...the "poop deck." I started to ask Louis if he knew why it was called that, but decided I really didn't want to know.

We went up two more flights of stairs and out onto the boat deck until we finally found the telegraph office. There was a notice on the door saying, "Keep Closed At All Times." That was no challenge for the three of us because we walked right through the door and started snooping around to see if we could find any evidence that Belle had been there. As we looked around the telegraph office, we saw the nervous little man Louis described, standing at the counter talking to himself as he sorted through two stacks of messages.

"I'll never get all these out on time! Why do people have to send all these useless telegrams just so they can brag that they're on a cruise ship?" he mumbled.

Cynthia and I took a moment to snicker, then got down to the business of trying to locate Belle's telegram. It appeared from the way the fidgety telegraph operator was working that one stack had already been sent and the other stack hadn't. Now to figure out how to sort through them without causing the kind of commotion we did in the dining room.

Suddenly an idea popped into my head. "Did you notice how windy it was out on deck?"

"Yeah, so what? We're probably cruising across the ocean at about thirty miles per hour, remember?" Cynthia answered absently.

"That's thirty *knots*, Miss Know-It-All." I

looked at Louis and he nodded affirmatively. "And if you're interested, I was thinking that if we could open the door just a little, the wind would blow these telegrams all over the room and it wouldn't be as obvious that we were going through them. This guy will be so busy trying to keep everything from blowing away, he won't have the chance to notice us at all."

"Well, it's about time you came up with a good idea," Cynthia said. "I'm impressed."

Although I noted a hint of sarcasm in her voice, I still took it as a sign that she thought it was worth a try, so I walked over and used my newfound power of concentration to slowly inch open the door. It just took a moment for the wind to start whipping through the small room, and for papers to start flying everywhere.

"Oh, no!" The poor man ran around the room in sheer panic as he tried to catch all the flying telegrams.

"Kind of gives a new meaning to the term *air mail* doesn't it?" I couldn't resist.

Cynthia ignored my feeble pun and started grabbing telegrams in mid-air, then started crawling around looking at every message that had floated to the floor, hoping to see a message from Belle. We must've gone through almost a hundred before finally spotting her name. The telegram read

On board ship STOP
Looking forward to a long visit STOP

Taking train from New York STOP
Will arrive at your home in two weeks STOP
Love, Belle

We slipped out of the room, leaving the poor telegraph officer sitting on the floor with a dazed look on his face. I felt sorry for him, but we had a mission and nothing was going to get in our way.

"One question, Sherlock," I asked. "How do we know whether Belle's telegram got sent or not?"

"We don't," Cynthia stated. "But since there were two stacks, there's a fifty-fifty chance it did, and besides, what difference will it make? If it wasn't sent, then Nana Anna and the rest of the family will be in for a big surprise."

"Makes as much sense as anything else around here," I said, relieved that my idea had been a success and that Cynthia didn't seem to be on her high horse anymore. "At least now we know for sure that Aunt Belle is on board, and all we have to do is find her before she runs into Andre…or he runs into her."

"I have to go find my dad," Louis blurted out looking at the clock on the wall. "We have dinner together every night."

"Uh, okay, Louis," I said reluctantly, since I'd grown kinda used to having a "little brother" hanging around. "Hey, why don't we go with you?" I said eagerly. "I mean it's not like your dad will notice a couple more invisible kids."

"Sure," Louis said enthusiastically. "It's this

way to his quarters. We'll go see it he's still there."

We followed Louis into a maze of hallways, and finally came to an impressive-looking stateroom door. Louis floated right through, and we jumped in behind him.

No one was there, so it gave us a chance to look around. "Wow," I said, gazing at the dark wood-paneled walls on which several richly framed paintings of sailing ships and old maps were hung. "Your dad must be important." On one wall sat a huge wooden keyhole desk covered with neat stacks of official-looking papers and a quill pen and ink well. On the other wall was a maroon leather-upholstered daybed with storage underneath.

"Yeah, Louis," Cynthia playfully tousled his hair, "for such a little squirt, your dad sure is a big guy."

Louis's chest puffed out visibly as he led us into another room. "He even has his own sleeping quarters," he announced proudly.

The first thing I immediately noticed was the light flowing in from two large portholes. Now this is my kind of cabin! No claustrophobia problems here. A double bed, two nightstands, and a large dresser rounded out the room. I turned to speak to Louis, but he'd already scampered back into his dad's office and was standing by the desk, staring intently.

"What are you doing?" I asked inquisitively. "Trying to stare a hole in that drawer?"

"Kind of," he answered sadly. "My old yo-yo is in there. My dad gave it to me on my last birthday…well, the last one that I was alive."

"Hey, cool, Louis," Cynthia exclaimed. "Let's see it."

He turned toward her, frustration evident on his face. "I can't open the drawer."

Cynthia and I looked at each other and smiled knowingly. "I think we can help," Cynthia said. "We had that same problem, but you can do it…if you really concentrate."

Louis looked unconvinced, but said, "Okay, so what do I have to do?"

"Just watch and learn," I commanded.

I stood at the desk and focused, my hand hovering just over the shiny, brass drawer handle, and repeated, "Open the drawer…open the drawer…open…the…drawer." The drawer not only opened, it flew out with such force that my hand almost flew off in the process. "Ow!" I laughed. "See, Louis? You *can* do it. Just make sure your hand is out of the way when you do."

"But I don't have to open it now! There's the yo-yo," he shouted.

I slowly stopped his hand from reaching into the drawer and said patiently, "No, Louis, you have to learn to do it yourself." Then, to his dismay, I closed the drawer, and once again his favorite toy was out of reach.

He sighed, "I'll try," and moved into position.

"Just concentrate," I said. "Imagine your hand actually touching the handle and pulling the drawer open."

He reached out hesitantly and started repeating, "Open the drawer..." To his delight, the drawer popped open, he grabbed the precious yo-yo, and smiled the biggest smile I'd ever seen. "I can't believe it." He shook his head, "I never thought I'd ever hold it again." Then he went on to tell us that every night before his dad went to bed, Louis would see him take it out of the desk and hold it lovingly in his hand. "Sometimes he'd smile, but most of the time I'd see tears in his eyes," Louis said sadly.

"Don't you have somewhere to go?" Cynthia interrupted him. "You're going to be late for dinner if you don't hurry."

"Yeah, Louis, you'd better get going. Will we see you again?" I asked as he turned toward the door.

"Sure," he replied cheerfully, already spinning the yo-yo up and down on its string. "I'll be around. See ya." And he vaporized right before our eyes.

Cynthia's Attic: The Missing Locket

Chapter Fifteen

Cynthia and I walked all the way around the deck hoping we might spot Belle among the hundreds of passengers sitting in deck chairs or standing at the rail looking out at the vast ocean. Although we were far from port, people never seemed to tire of watching the waves or spotting an occasional dolphin or sailfish jump out of the water. It all looked pretty boring to me.

After scouting out the main deck of the ship without spotting Belle, we went back inside and decided to search for the passenger list. As we entered through the doors, we heard the distinct sounds of classical music coming from below. Descending the Grand Staircase, we discovered a five-piece orchestra playing for the enjoyment of a small group of passengers in the main lounge. Another group was standing just to the right of the orchestra, staring intently into the middle of the crowd. Since we weren't much into violin music, we walked over to the other group (we actually walked right through them) to find a beautiful young woman sitting in a chair posing for a portrait painted by the rude man who'd pushed his way onto the ship. It was Andre.

We could finally put a face to the stories we'd heard from Belle, and didn't feel good about what we saw. Andre's hair, along with his very distinctive slashing eyebrows, full beard, and mustache, were coal black. His skin was very fair, almost to the point of looking unhealthy, even dead, and his thin lips were curved slightly upward in a sly smirk directed at the young lady he was painting. But as I watched his expert brushstrokes on the canvas in front of him, I glanced at Cynthia and said, grudgingly, "You know, he really is good."

"Yeah," she replied resentfully. "And he sure looks like he's enjoying himself. Do you think that's how he looked at Aunt Belle when he painted her portrait?"

She no sooner had Belle's name out of her mouth than Andre quickly looked up as if he'd heard her. Cynthia and I gasped as we stared straight into his gray, shark-cold eyes, and were frozen to the floor as he appeared to stare directly back at us. Then, after what seemed like hours, he shrugged and looked back at his subject, continuing to paint as if nothing had happened. Our shoulders dropped as we both sighed with relief, but still felt very uneasy as to whether he'd actually been able to hear us talking about Belle.

We might never know, but the important thing was that we'd located Belle's painter. From the sound of the threats Belle said that he'd made the last time they were together, and our first uneasy encounter with him, we were convinced we couldn't let him anywhere near her.

Walking back through the crowd, we happened to notice the purser's office was empty, which might be the perfect time for us to see if we could find a passenger list. Walking through the wall, we started our search for Belle's cabin number.

"Here's the list," Cynthia said as she tried to open the ship's manifest. She was having the same trouble I'd had with the apple.

"Concentrate, Cynthia. You can do it."

Finally, after almost staring holes in the book, she was able to open it and start looking down each page. "There sure are a lot of people on board," she said, going through page after page. "Here it is! Belle's name! She's on D deck, cabin 24. Let's go find her."

Running down several flights of steps, we found her cabin without much difficulty, but decided to knock first instead of just barging in on her.

"Whoops," I laughed. "You can't make any noise on a door when your fist goes right through it."

Not wanting to waste all that time and energy trying to knock, we decided to listen at the door, but didn't hear anyone stirring around in the cabin.

"She could be asleep. Why don't you just tiptoe in and make sure she's not there before we go on a wild goose chase," I said impatiently. "I'll stay out here and watch for her." My plan was to get rid of

Cynthia for a few minutes so I could snoop in the cabin across the hall while she looked around in Belle's.

But she went through the door and then came back out after only a few seconds, before I even had the chance to move. "Well, that was fast," I said, a little annoyed.

"Have you ever been in one of those cabins?" she asked. "It's not much bigger than my closet. If I'd stayed much longer I would've gotten claustrophobia. Believe me, no one's in there."

We made our way back to the main lounge, but the crowds of people had disappeared for the most part. A very elegant-looking couple walked past us discussing the dinner menu for that evening, so we decided to follow them into the dining room. After my unfortunate "apple incident," I promised Cynthia I would touch *nothing*.

While sauntering down the hallway, I said confidently, "I'll bet we find Belle in the dining room, because if she's on board, she'll have to eat, won't she?"

"I hope so," Cynthia said. "Just make sure *you* don't!"

We came to a long line of people waiting to get into the dining room, and after seeing that Belle wasn't standing there, we walked through the doors and began our search.

"You start on that side, and I'll take this one," Cynthia motioned. "And if you spot her, don't make a scene. I don't know if she'll be able to see us or not."

Hmmm…I never thought about that. Would Belle even know we were here?

I started at the very end of the huge dining room and slowly made my way from table to table, looking carefully at every single person. I spotted Louis sitting at the captain's table. Hmmm, that's strange. He's sitting in what must be an empty chair, right beside his dad. I can't understand why some important passenger wouldn't be assigned the seat beside the captain. No time to worry about an empty chair, though. I have work to do.

The nightly meals were being brought out from the kitchen on dining trays, and then would be placed on the tables. Each individual meal had a cover over it, but the aroma was driving me crazy! Maybe I could just take the lid off one of them and sample…No! Cynthia would kill me if I caused another food scene.

After getting my mind back on the business at hand, I looked up just in time to see Cynthia waving frantically from the other end of the room. She'd spotted Aunt Belle.

When I reached the table where Belle was sitting, I could see that she was having a very enjoyable conversation with a young man about her age. There was no doubt from the look on his face that he was enjoying talking to her too. A full head of sandy-colored hair framed his dazzling green eyes. As we listened to him talk, his distinctly British accent was soft and friendly. There were three other couples at the table, but Belle and the young man didn't seem to notice them, and not only that, Belle had no idea we were standing beside her.

I poked Cynthia and whispered, "So what do you think we should do? Stand guard over Aunt Belle for the rest of the trip?"

Cynthia whispered back, "I don't know what good it'll do. If she doesn't even know we're here, how are we going to be able to protect her? And why are we whispering?"

I shrugged my shoulders and pointed at two empty chairs that were pulled out at the next table. We slid discreetly onto the seats and waited while Belle and her dinner companion finished their entrée, dessert, and coffee. My eyes were immediately drawn to a plate of fancy cookies sitting right at my fingertips. Cynthia must've read my thoughts because, without even looking my way, I heard her hiss, "*Don't...even...think about it.*"

After a while, Belle and the young man got up from the table, said their goodbyes to the other six people at the table, and strolled out of the dining room with us hot on their heels. We weren't sure what we were protecting her from, or how we were going to do it, but we weren't going to let her out of our sight.

On my way out the door, I turned toward Louis, and mouthed the words, "See you later." He waved back, perfectly content to sit at the table and watch the captain eat dinner while he dutifully talked to the people who'd been invited to join him for the evening.

Following closely behind Belle and her companion, we heard that he was a musician from London named Michael. He'd recently played violin for the London Symphony and was going to New York for an audition. He told Belle that although he had family and security in England, his dream had always been to go to America, and if his audition didn't work out in New York, he'd move on to Boston or Philadelphia. Cynthia and I felt kind of funny eavesdropping, but we knew of no other way to keep our eyes on Belle. Besides, we liked this guy and thought they were great together.

The four of us moved out onto the deck and Michael told Belle about his family. His mother and father were both stage actors and he had three younger sisters. They hated to see him go, but knew he had to follow his dream.

"That's quite enough about me, Belle," Michael insisted. "Tell me about you."

Belle hesitated as if she were trying to decide just how much to tell him about Andre and the reason she was escaping to America. Finally she began cautiously, "I was a dancer in Paris, but gave it up several years ago. I'm only now realizing what a mistake it was, because I gave up my dream for someone I thought loved me...and now he's gone and so is the dream."

Michael gently put his hand on her shoulder and said, "It's never too late, Belle. I can't imagine any dance company in the world that would turn you away."

Belle said that she wasn't sure she had the confidence or the strength to audition again, and quickly changed the subject to her sister Anna and the family that was awaiting her visit. They talked for what seemed like hours, and just when we were getting very bored with all the grownup conversation, Belle yawned, "I'm getting a little tired and should probably say goodnight. Maybe we can have breakfast together in the morning."

"I'd love that, Belle," Michael said. They made plans to meet that next day.

Finally saying goodnight, Belle walked back to her cabin with the two of us trailing behind. "Gus, listen. Aunt Belle is actually whistling."

She was not only whistling, she was almost skipping down the hallway to her cabin. "I think she's finally getting over her awful experience with Andre. I don't understand what she saw in him anyway," I said disgustedly. "Now if we can just keep her from running into him."

The words were no sooner spoken than we saw a blur leap out of the shadows at the same moment we heard a muffled scream come from Belle. It was Andre, and his tone of voice was anything but friendly.

Chapter Sixteen

"Don't scream, Belle," Andre threatened. "I won't hurt you. I just want to talk." With his hand over Belle's mouth while twisting her arm behind her back as he pushed her up the hallway, it was impossible to believe that he "just wanted to talk."

"Now, when we go out on deck, you're going to let me explain what happened in Paris. Are you going to give me another chance?" he snarled through clenched teeth.

Belle just nodded her head, since she had no way of speaking. But even though she agreed to listen, Cynthia and I could see the fear in her eyes.

"What are we going to do?" Cynthia cried.

"Let's just follow them. He said he wasn't going to hurt her. Maybe he really does want to talk to her," I said, hoping I sounded more convincing than I felt.

Fortunately, there was no indication that Andre felt our presence as we followed them down the hallway and up the stairs to the main deck. He no longer had his hand over her mouth, but the deep impressions of his fingernails on her forearm said it all. They walked to the stern of the ship, then down the stairs to the boat deck. Cynthia and I kept praying that someone would come along to see that Belle was in trouble, but the night air was so cold that everyone had either gone to their cabins or were enjoying the entertainment being held inside the ship.

Unexpectedly, Andre stopped and pulled Belle to the railing in between two of the lifeboats.

We heard Belle ask anxiously, "Andre, what has happened to you? You look so thin and pale. Have you been ill?"

"I became *ill* the day you walked out of my life," Andre sneered, "and never recovered." Then his voice became even lower and more threatening as he continued, "I told you one day you'd be sorry for not giving me a second chance, Isabelle, and that day has come."

"Gus," Cynthia screamed. "He's going to throw her overboard! We have to do something!"

Without thinking, I lunged for Andre…and went right through him and almost through the railing. I tried once more, barely catching myself before falling into the black, churning sea. Why couldn't I do this? I must be too scared to concentrate. As I regained my balance, I saw that he had his hand over Belle's mouth again and was pulling her ever closer to the railing. All we could hear were her muffled screams.

"We can't stop him," I yelled.

The look on Cynthia's face made shivers run down my spine. "Oh yes we can," she answered coldly. She'd spotted one of the large wooden oars that were resting on the closest lifeboat. Clearing her mind of everything but the oar, she was able to grab it with both hands as she fixed her gaze squarely on Andre.

"You're not throwing my aunt over the side of this boat," she yelled, swinging with all the might her eighty-pound body could gather. Somehow, someway...she made solid contact, knocking him out cold and into the lifeboat. I stood by in stunned silence...and Belle passed out on the deck.

Finally snapping out of my daze, I ran over to look after Belle as Cynthia tiptoed to the lifeboat and peered in at Andre. "He's unconscious." She sighed with relief, still gripping the oar tightly. "And I plan to see that he stays that way until someone comes along to help Belle."

"Cynthia, look around," I moaned. "No one's going to come out here until morning. I'll see if I can find a way to get someone's attention." I took off, unsure what I was going to accomplish, but if Cynthia can swing an oar that was double her size and knock a full-grown man into a lifeboat...hey, I can surely find help for Belle.

I walked all the way around the deck, but no one was outside. Ready to give up, I spotted a very distinguished-looking man coming out one of the doors wearing an equally distinguished-looking white uniform covered with tons of gold braiding. It was the captain...Louis's dad. Considering his rank and very large stature, I knew he'd be the best person to protect Belle, and put Andre someplace where he wouldn't be able to hurt her again.

I ran to him and started talking a mile a minute. "Please sir. You have to come with me. There's a horrible man who's going to throw my best friend's aunt overboard!"

Stupid! That's not going to work! He can't possibly hear me, so what now? Maybe if I jump up and down and poke him with my finger... Still no response. So I kicked him in the shin as hard as I could. He flinched, but I could see that kicking wasn't going to be enough unless I could get him to follow me. That's when I noticed the hat he was clutching to keep it from blowing off his head. Hmmm...if I could just get that hat.

I took a couple of steps backward and leaped, pretending I was snagging a high fly ball in one of our neighborhood softball games, and soared off the ground just high enough to snatch the hat from the captain's head. I took off running...with him in close pursuit.

I twirled the hat around, dragging it on the deck a few times just out of his reach so it would appear to be carried off by the wind. I juggled it from one hand to the other, and whenever he'd get a little too close, I'd start running as if it had just been captured by a big gust.

"Hey, that looks like fun!"

"Louis," I gasped, "Don't jump out at me like

that!"

"Oh, sorry." He chuckled. "It's just that I'm still trying to communicate with my dad, and nothing seems to work." Looking back at the captain huffing and puffing behind us as he attempted to catch up with his hat, Louis added with a laugh, "*You* sure have his attention."

"Yeah, Louis, and I have to *keep* it," I panted impatiently, "…so don't distract me. I have to get your dad to help Aunt Belle. She's in terrible trouble." Louis dropped behind me and ran along beside his dad while I continued to bob and weave down the deck toward the lifeboats.

Louis's laughter made me wish I'd been able to see just how silly the captain looked running after his flying hat, but I didn't have time to play games at the moment because of my fear for Belle's safety.

We finally reached the lifeboat and Andre. He was still out cold, but Belle was holding her head and trying to figure out why she was sitting on the deck.

"What happened, Miss?" the captain asked as he bent down to retrieve the "wayward" hat that I'd placed at Belle's feet. "Did you fall?"

"I…I…don't know. I must have passed out." Frantically, Belle looked up. "Where's Andre? There was a man out here threatening me, and…and…I think he was trying to throw me off the ship!"

But as she spoke, the captain was already

peering into the lifeboat. "You mean the gentleman lying here in this boat? I don't think he's going to give you any trouble for awhile."

Belle shakily stood, walked over to the lifeboat, and looked in at Andre. "That's the man, and I assure you he's no gentleman…but how did he get in there?"

The Captain looked at Belle, and then down at the oar that was now lying on the deck, and said with obvious amazement, "You tell me. Either you knocked him in there yourself or you have a guardian angel."

Cynthia and I looked at each other and collapsed on the deck from exhaustion, but most of all from relief that Belle was finally safe.

"You two were great," Louis acknowledged. "I didn't think *girls* were that strong."

"Why, you little pipsqueak!" Cynthia jumped to her feet, forgetting her exhaustion. "How would you like to take a flying leap into that lifeboat with Andre?"

Louis backed away quickly, laughing, "I was just kidding. You really were great. I'm glad I met both of you," he added, sincerely.

That soothed Cynthia's feelings and we gave him a relieved hug and sat back down on the deck.

"You really impressed me, Cynthia," I said, with genuine admiration.

"Hey, you weren't so bad yourself, Gus," she said, giving me a good-natured shove.

The captain summoned help, took a statement, and then escorted Belle back to her cabin with Louis skipping along behind. Meanwhile, Andre, who was starting to come out of his "oar-induced sleep," was handcuffed and thrown into the ship's brig. He wouldn't be bothering Belle or anyone else for the rest of the voyage.

The next few days were uneventful, thank goodness. Due to Michael's constant attention, Belle quickly recovered from her experience on the boat deck. Michael was horrified at what had happened, and blamed himself for not seeing Belle safely to her cabin that night.

"I'm so sorry, Belle, but you can be sure that as long as I'm around, no one will ever hurt you again."

Cynthia and I were relieved when we heard that statement. Now maybe we could relax and enjoy some ghostly mischief-making before the ship reached its destination.

Late one afternoon, while we were ducking in and out of the passenger cabins playing some harmless tricks such as packing clothes that had been laid out for dinner and then leaving the suitcases beside the cabin doors, we ran into Louis.

"Hey, *Louie*," I shouted, "where ya been?"

"I told you it's…oh, never mind," he laughed. "I wanted to see you before we docked so I could say goodbye."

"Goodbye? But you haven't finished your story," I said eagerly. "We still don't know how you ended up, uh, well…haunting this ship."

"Gus," Cynthia said sharply." Maybe he doesn't want to talk about it."

Louis looked up and grinned. "Oh, that's okay, I really don't mind. In fact, it might be nice to tell somebody. You're the first people I've been able to talk to since it happened."

"Since *what* happened?" I insisted.

"Let's go sit on the deck," he said, "and I'll tell you the whole story."

We knew that the captain had taken Louis on a voyage, against his mother's wishes, and that he'd died, probably from typhoid fever. We sat down on three empty deck chairs, and he continued the story. Two days had passed since his death when his father tearfully made the decision to bury him at sea, since going back to port was impossible. Louis's spirit watched as his father grieved and agonized over the fact that he'd brought him on the trip. *If only he'd listened to his wife.* No one could console him.

"It was then that I decided I couldn't leave. Somehow, I had to help him. Through time he's gotten better, but I'd like, just once more, to hear him laugh," Louis said softly. "He had the greatest laugh."

"Maybe we can help," I said enthusiastically. "It's almost dinnertime. Louis, we're going to help you make your dad laugh again. Follow me."

We walked into the formal dining room just as the passengers were strolling in and taking their seats.

"Okay, now what, Gus?" Cynthia asked, arms folded.

"Watch the Master," I said smugly.

"Oh, good grief," Cynthia muttered, plopping down on an empty chair.

I walked over to the closest table, swiped a large white napkin, and started running back and forth in between tables. I began to hear a low muttering among the diners, which then swelled to a few cries of, "What's going on? Is the wind blowing in here?" I looked at Louis and he had a little smile on his face. Even Cynthia had an uncontrollable smirk. "They haven't seen anything yet." I chuckled under my breath.

A long line of tuxedoed waiters was coming out of the kitchen into the dining room. I jumped onto a chair, and just as one of them passed by–his arm held high balancing a tray and a dome-covered plate–I opened the lid, grabbed a large, steamed lobster, and heaved the red crustacean as far as I could…right onto the very bad toupee of a pompous passenger. The startled man angrily grabbed the lobster…and off came his hair, clinging to the lobster claws as the mortified waiter ran over to assist. Cynthia and Louis couldn't contain themselves. They doubled over with laughter, along with the other diners at the table of the *suddenly bald* man.

Wiping the tears from her eyes, Cynthia said

appreciatively, "I have to hand it to you Gus, that was priceless."

"Yeah," Louis agreed, jumping up and down. "I haven't had this much fun in years!"

I noticed that the captain had been looking in our direction and observing the commotion, then his attention abruptly turned from the man who was trying to get his toupee untangled from his dinner, to Louis, who was absentmindedly spinning the yo-yo up and down, back and forth.

"Uh…Louis," I said slowly. "You might want to look at your dad."

Louis turned toward the captain's table and saw the most wondrous expression on his dad's face. It was a mixture of astonishment, disbelief, and elation. Louis slowly let the yo-yo wind back up in his hand, and walked toward his dad.

"C'mon." I grabbed Cynthia excitedly. "Let's go see what happens!"

"No, Gus," she answered. "Let's leave them alone."

I knew she was right. After all, they hadn't "seen" each other in more than five years. We watched as the captain pulled out the empty chair beside him, which we later learned had remained vacant since his son's death. As Louis sat down, he placed the yo-yo into his dad's outstretched hand. I don't know if the captain actually saw him, or just saw his son's favorite toy, but it was obvious he knew Louis had, in some form, come back to him.

As we turned to walk out of the dining room, knowing we'd accomplished enough for one evening, we heard spontaneous laughter coming from the head table. You could've heard a pin drop. The entire roomful of diners had stopped eating, drinking, and talking, and were watching wide-eyed as the captain chuckled and wiped tears of joy from his eyes. As I walked out the dining room door, I imagined the passengers were probably hoping that the commander of their ship hadn't suffered a nervous breakdown.

Although we were happy that we'd helped reunite Louis with his dad, another personally satisfying trick happened on the final day of the voyage. We spotted the portrait displayed in the reception area that Andre had painted our first day on the ship. A group of people was standing around admiring the work of the notorious painter who had tried to throw a young female passenger overboard.

"Ya know, Cynthia, since you and I are the ones who exposed Andre's evil deeds, don't you think we're obligated to add a few finishing touches to his painting?" As good as it was, we couldn't help but think there was something missing from the face of his lovely subject. With the interested crowd gathered around, the brush mysteriously rose from the easel, dipped itself in black paint, and started drawing a very large black mustache. There was a loud gasp. As the stunned group witnessed yet another strange occurrence, Cynthia and I stood there admiring our work and having a good laugh at Andre's expense.

But in spite of all the fun we had, even our best tricks seemed boring compared to the excitement that had taken place on the boat deck a few nights earlier.

After landing in New York, Belle walked happily off the ship hand-in-hand with Michael. Cynthia and I just stood near the gangplank listening to the anxious comments concerning all the strange happenings on the "ghost ship."

"But Miranda! I swear I didn't tie your nightgown to the railing outside the cabin!"

"Well then, who did...your dead Aunt Maude?"

We giggled, and then heard another couple behind us.

"I tell you, this ship is going to pay for my tuxedo! Why, when that flying lobster landed on my toupee, it's no wonder I spilled that drink in my lap trying to duck!"

"Oh, Henry. Loosen up! From my point of view, it's the only time during the whole voyage you showed any life, not to mention that you look much better without that silly *rug* on your head!"

We laughed out loud at that one, and were pleased that we'd not only saved Belle from certain death, but had also given everyone, including us, a trip to remember.

Oh, and as they were *escorting* Andre off the ship in handcuffs, Louis appeared once more and managed to speed up the prisoner's exit by sticking out his leg and tripping him as he walked by, causing the wicked artist to go tumbling head over heels down the gangplank.

"Hey, thanks, Louis. Take care. Why, we might even miss you," I said with a chuckle.

"Happy to help," he replied. "It's the least I can do after what you've done for me."

"So, your dad finally knows you're here, right?" I asked.

"He feels my presence," Louis answered. "He laughed when I put the yo-yo in his hands, so I think he's ready to accept my death and move on with his life. And don't worry...I imagine he thinks I'm the one who threw the lobster on that old man's head the other night," he added.

"Maybe with practice, kid, you can get as good at causing trouble as we are," I said proudly. "At least we've taught you everything we know. Now, it's up to you."

Louis laughed. "I don't want to cause my dad *too* much trouble, and now that I'm pretty sure he's going to be okay, who knows...I may drop in on *you* someday," he added playfully.

"That would be great," I said sincerely, "but try not to sneak up on us the next time."

With the promise of a future visit from our new friend, we waved goodbye and then, as we happily took one step off the ship, we were back in Clara's attic.

Chapter Seventeen

"Well," I sighed, completely worn out, "so much for having a boring summer. Although that was a little too much excitement even if it's the only time in my life I'll ever be able to take a trip across the ocean without getting seasick."

"Yeah, well, the only trip I want to take right now is the trip back home," Cynthia said wearily. "Any ideas?"

Before I could suggest giving the trunk another try, we heard a disturbance coming from downstairs.

"Oh, not again," I groaned. I was too tired to take any more excitement, but shrugged my shoulders and sighed, "Might as well check it out."

As we reached the foyer, we were thrilled to see that all the commotion was coming from Clara, Nana Anna, and...Belle. There were so many hugs, kisses, and tears that we lost count, and would've given anything to be able to join in the complete and total joy of the moment. Of course that was impossible since, to the three of them, we weren't even there. Still, we decided to stick around and enjoy their happiness at being reunited.

Belle and Anna sat at the table drinking tea and talking for hours, with Clara sitting alongside taking in every single word. Belle told them the same story we'd heard about breaking up with Andre, and then the terrifying experience at the lifeboat.

"I just wish I knew who knocked Andre into that boat," Belle began. "The captain thought I'd done it and then passed out from fright, but I had a feeling someone was watching over me that night, and whoever it was saved my life."

Cynthia and I looked at each other with a true sense of accomplishment. Not only had we brought Louis and his dad back together, we'd saved the locket from being lost forever and then saved Belle from being tossed into the sea. Who cares if no one knew but us…*we* knew, and that's what counted.

"Oh, Belle," Anna sighed. "I'm so sorry about what happened, but even more sorry that you had to go through all that misery alone. If only I'd known, I would've gone to Paris in the beginning and dragged you home so your family could've taken care of you. Then that horrible Andre wouldn't have been able to get near you on that ship!"

"Ha!" Belle laughed scornfully at Anna's statement. "You, little sister, would've had a real fight on your hands. I was in no mood during that awful time to be around people who would just sit around feeling sorry for me, and I don't want pity now. In fact, that's the last thing I need. But," she went on to say, "no need to argue about it now. I'm here for a good long visit, and I'm not going to leave until the whole unpleasant experience is completely out of my mind."

We also found out that, before the train trip that brought her here, Belle had spent several days in New York with Michael and had set up an audition with the ballet when she returned to the city. Cynthia and I were happy about the audition and thrilled that she was going to be seeing more of Michael. But something was bothering me.

"*Hmmm.* It sounds like it took her almost a week to get here. Where did all the time go?"

"I don't know," Cynthia sighed. "We stepped off the boat and were in Clara's attic just moments before Belle arrived. I guess it's not important–Belle's safe and so are we."

Belle then turned to Clara and said, "You're just as I pictured you. We've spent hours talking about me...now I want to find out about your life."

Clara looked pleased and spent the next hour telling Aunt Belle about school and about her friends, especially Bess, until Belle interrupted. "Anna. I have a great idea. Unless you object, I'd like Clara to have my locket. That is, if you think she's responsible enough to take care of it."

Cynthia and I practically choked when we heard that. If they only knew how much trouble we'd gone through in order to save the locket *and* Clara's neck!

"I don't know, Belle," Anna said thoughtfully. "Maybe we should wait for a few years until Clara can truly understand the sentimental value of the locket and learn to take care of it."

As we all waited for Clara to whine and beg her mother to let her have the locket now, she said something that surprised everyone in the room, including us. "I appreciate the thought, Aunt Belle, but I think Mother's right. I'm not sure why, but something tells me I should wait until I'm older before taking on the responsibility of the locket. That way I know it will always be in a safe place until the right time comes."

Nana Anna, expecting to have a huge fight on her hands, was too amazed by Clara's attitude to speak, but Belle said, "Whatever you wish, Clara. Just remember, the locket will be yours until you decide to pass it on to your daughter or perhaps even your granddaughter." As she said this, Cynthia looked at me and smiled, probably dreaming of the day that Mama Clara would hand the locket over to her.

Cynthia and I spent as much time as we dared at Clara's house that day. Bess stopped by to meet the famous dancer, and we finally got to hear all the stories we'd hoped to hear at Aunt Belle's cottage. It was also nice seeing such a different side to Nana Anna. She'd been so stern and unhappy when we'd been at Clara's house after the locket had been lost, that seeing her talk and laugh now made it clear how much her sister, Belle, meant to her life. Not only that, we saw a completely different side to our grandmothers. They weren't just the comfortable

old grannies we'd grown to love in their later years–
they'd actually been a couple of fun-loving, giggling
girls just like us. And Clara was able to show Bess
the locket without getting into serious trouble.

As much as we enjoyed the conversations, we
knew it was time to go up to the attic and try to find
our way back home. At about the same time, Bess
and Clara said goodnight to Aunt Belle and Nana
Anna, and walked upstairs just in front of us. Bess
was going to spend the night and I'm sure that
neither one of them was going to get much sleep,
considering the events of the day.

We'd just opened the door to the attic when we
heard Bess's voice coming from Clara's bedroom,
"Clara, do you want to have some *real* fun on
Saturday?"

"Doing what?" Clara asked suspiciously.

"I overheard my father telling Mama that he was
going to be delivering an organ to the circus in Tell
City," Bess said excitedly, "and I'm going with him."

"But I didn't think your mother ever let you go
on those trips, Bess. What changed her mind?"
Clara asked.

"Uh, well…she doesn't exactly know about it.
As a matter of fact, *Papa* isn't going to know either.
I'm going to sneak into the organ crate after it's
loaded onto the wagon, and he won't find me until
after we get there."

"Bess! That could be dangerous, and besides,
he's going to be really mad when he finds out what

you've done," Clara warned.

"Maybe at first," Bess admitted, "but he won't be mad for long, and then I know I can talk him into letting me stay for the circus. Oh, please say you'll go with me, Clara."

"No, it sounds too risky to me," Clara said, a little disappointment in her voice. "And besides, Aunt Belle will still be here and Mother said we're going to the Meyer's farm for a picnic that day."

"A boring picnic? Clara, where's your spirit of adventure?" Bess said impatiently.

"Sorry," Clara stated. "I just don't want to spend the day riding in a stuffy old organ crate in the back of a wagon!"

"Well, just stay home then, and when I get back I'll be sure to tell you about the clowns and trapeze artists and, who knows, I may even get to ride an elephant," Bess said haughtily.

"An elephant?" Clara exclaimed. "Well, maybe I can get out of the picnic."

I looked at Cynthia and nodded my head. "That kinda sounds like fun to me too. I'd love to spend the day getting to know my great-grandfather. Wish we could figure out a way to go check out that circus, and maybe find a way to keep Clara and Bess from getting into too much trouble."

Cynthia agreed. "It could be a fun way to spend the day, but I have no idea how we'd get there. Do you?" Before I could answer, she rambled on, "Who knows...we may just have to wait until we uncover an "invitation" before we can go with them. I hope we do, because I have a feeling those two will need watching or they might just go flying off the wagon, along with the organ, before they even reach the circus. Besides, you really should find a way to return your grandmother's clothes."

It seemed so strange to think about trying to keep our grandmothers out of trouble, but after the experience with Andre and Belle, we'd grown up well beyond our years. As we made our way slowly up to the attic, we talked about how much we wanted to be back in the safety and comfort of our own homes, although we were going to miss Clara, Bess, Nana Anna, and especially Aunt Belle. It had been an amazing adventure–one that we wouldn't soon forget.

The trunk looked shiny and new, the way it had before the first trip to Clara's house. That must be a good sign. We carefully opened it and saw a note lying right on top. It read: *I'll stay in touch, Love, Aunt Belle.* After changing back into the ballet costume and the sailor dress and leaving Clara and Bess's clothes tucked safely in the trunk, we were, thankfully, on our way home.

We were tired and a little confused, but safely back in Cynthia's attic. We sat there for a few minutes trying to decide if our journey had been a dream or just a product of our very vivid imaginations. After deciding that neither one of us had an imagination *that* good, we knew there was only one way to find out for sure–we had to see Mama Clara. Cynthia carefully took off the ballet costume and I slid out of the sailor dress, just in case we might need them again. But as I folded the dress, I felt something in the pocket that I hadn't noticed before. Reaching in, I pulled out a strange-looking card.

"Look at this, Cynthia," I said. "It doesn't look like any card I've ever seen." I glanced at the strange markings, and then handed it to her.

"It looks like one of those cards that Gypsies use to tell fortunes," she said. "Don't they usually have fortune tellers at the circus?"

"*Hmmm*…maybe they do. But we can look at it later," I said, a little preoccupied as I put the card back where I found it. "First, we need to go see your grandmother."

As soon as we were dressed in our own comfortable clothes, we headed for Mama Clara's.

The house was eerily silent as we walked in and noticed that most of the lights were off. After searching every room, and getting ready to leave, I spotted Mama Clara sitting in her rocking chair fast asleep. Cynthia walked over to her grandmother and started to cover her with an afghan when I heard her whisper, "Gus, come here and look." I quietly walked over to the rocking chair. In Mama Clara's hand was a bell-shaped locket. Cynthia smiled and then pointed to a picture we'd never seen before that was sitting on the bookcase behind the rocker–a picture of Belle, Michael, and their *three children*. We'd changed the past more than we realized, and it looked like in the near future, Cynthia might be busy getting acquainted with her cousins–Belle's great- grandchildren.

We walked silently out of the house so we wouldn't wake Mama Clara, and went back to Cynthia's.

As we made our way up the walk to the kitchen door, I turned to her and said, "I sure hope my grandmother doesn't get into as much trouble as Aunt Belle and Mama Clara. But from what we've seen so far, I have a feeling we'll need to get plenty of rest if we decide to take that trip to the circus."

Epilogue

On several occasions following our discovery of the note from Belle that was pinned to the ballet dress, we swore we heard dancing coming from the attic above Cynthia's room. We also took several more trips, including our amazing adventure at the circus with Clara and Bess...but that's another story.

Meet the Author:

Mary and her husband, Ken, live in Ft. Myers, FL, and are the parents of three grown children…and Molly, their beloved, adopted canine.

She is co-author of a humorous lifestyle book, and is published in the Gulf Coast Writers Anthology, Vol. VI.

The idea for the *Cynthia's Attic* series came about through the recurring dream of a mysterious attic. Upon realizing that the dream took place in the Southern Indiana home of her childhood friend, Cynthia, the dreams stopped, and the writing began.

When she isn't dodging hurricanes, Mary enjoys swimming, bike riding, and the Southwest Florida Beaches.

Also available from Echelon Press Publishing

Pretty, Pretty (*Young Adult Mystery*) K.C. Oliver

Quinn and Holly have landed the summer job of a lifetime; working in *Hawaii!* With great weather, beautiful scenery, and cute guys...it's a job to die for...literally. But with the help of new friend, Jaxon, they begin to uncover the horror behind the mysterious hotel. Only someone or something doesn't want them to learn the truth, and will stop at nothing to make sure that the only place they will be taking any secrets; is to their *graves!*

$9.99   ISBN 1-59080-253-5

Trails of the Dime Novel (*Western Adventure*) Terry Burns

Danger and excitement...In the late 1800's the imagination of a nation was fueled by the wonder of Dime Novels. Gunfights and showdowns...Rick Dayton is headed west to write the beloved stories only to find himself living them instead. The making of legends...Travel across the west with him as every new adventure offers another novel in the journey of a lifetime.

$13.99   ISBN 1-59080-386-8

Anna Chase and the Butterfly Girls (*Fantasy for Young Readers*) Jadan B. Grace

Anna Chase is thrilled to share the tales of the Butterfly Girls with her young daughter, Brandy. Stories of another time and place offer solace to the lonely heart of the young widow as she relives the triumphs and tragedies of the beautiful winged creatures. Day by day, Anna tells the story of the exquisite Lady Willow and handsome Baron of Butterfly Haven who triumph over drought and devastation.

$10.99   ISBN 1-59080-083-4

True Friends (*Historical for Young Readers*) Grace E. Howell

In 1918 Memphis, Annie's carefree days of softball with the boys are nearly gone, but not forgotten. Now she must learn to be a "proper" girl. Discouraged, she falls under the spell of the new girl on the block. Iris Elizabeth introduces her to a world of silk dresses, the theater, and school popularity. But Iris Elizabeth has a dark side, and she pressures Annie to give up her old friends. Confused by the things Iris knows, Annie wonders, can it be true? Are Rose and Della Bolman really Huns? And could their father be a German spy?

$9.99   ISBN 1-59080-420-1